To SHMILY

Happy Holidays

The
Spoiled Child

T. Arthur Engard

iUniverse, Inc.
New York   Bloomington

The Spoiled Child

iUniverse books may be ordered through booksellers or by contacting:

iUniverse
1663 Liberty Drive
Bloomington, IN 47403
www.iuniverse.com
1-800-Authors (1-800-288-4677)

ISBN: 978-1-4401-7635-7 (pbk)
ISBN: 978-1-4401-7636-4 (ebk)

Library of Congress Control Number: 2009937235

Printed in the United States of America

iUniverse rev. date: 9/24/2009

CHAPTER 1
The Spoiled Child

First of all, I must tell you my child is not spoiled. I should know, I am his mother. He is merely strong-willed. He can be difficult at times, but all-in-all he is an adorable if not obedient child. I will thank you not to repeat what you might have heard from the town gossips.

You need only look at last Christmas season for an example. There were so many instances that demonstrated how loving and considerate my son could be. His noble and well-mannered nature is always most evident during the Christmas season.

Christmas! It is a season we look forward to all year. A season of joy that underscores the good fortune with which we've been blessed. My husband, God rest his soul, began many of the traditions we still observe as a family: my mother, my son and myself. Even now, three years after my mister's untimely death, we find delight in all the Yuletide activities and decorations that were once his.

Last year my son was just learning his letters. He would continuously ask me how to spell the names of toys he expected for Christmas. He had made several lists by the time Thanksgiving arrived. I was a bit dismayed at the number of toys on the lists. My husband had left a sizable endowment, but it would not last long if I spent so much on playthings for the boy. I tried hiding the lists, but alas his memory was quite good and he would just rewrite them, adding more as he went.

Oh, but this little anxiety could not dampen my joy of the season! I began decorating the house the day after Thanksgiving as I always do. Cherished ornaments, wreaths, and stockings were hung as my child pointed to where they should go. He would eventually get tired of directing the work and would go play elsewhere, at which time I would stop also. If I continued and hung an ornament in a place of which my child disapproved, there would ensue a tantrum of one sort or another. It was much easier to avoid the conflict altogether. I did on one occasion, however, hang a wreath on the outside of the front door while he played at hoop in the yard.

'It should go on the inside, Mummy,' he said to me. 'I can't see it when I'm playing inside.'

'It always goes here, little man,' I began. 'A wreath is a greeting...'

'INSIDE!' he had said in a loud voice. I saw Mrs. Mestik peek out of her curtain next door. I attempted to head off a tantrum which would add fuel to the neighborhood gossip.

'Time to go in for a wash,' I had said to him, glancing at Mrs. Mestik's window. You'd have thought I said I was going to boil him in a cauldron. He screamed and ran down the street. There was no avoiding a scene at that point. I hiked up my skirts, chased and caught him by the arm. I had to drag him, kicking and screaming all the way, into the house.

In my mortification, I shut him in his room. He kicked the door for a full twenty minutes screaming how much he hated me. I must tell you that that my child didn't mean this. He merely wanted to show me his anger. I am sure he realized how privileged he was, living in a fine house with his Mother's love to please him.

So it was that it took me three days to put the house in proper Christmas attire that year. How beautiful it looked! By the front door stood Mr. And Mrs. Santa with rosy porcelain faces. Delicately embroidered stockings hung from the hearth. The collection of music boxes that played Christmas carols sat on the piano. There were nutcrackers standing at attention with painted grins on several tables, dolls dressed as carolers in the curio cabinet, and a priceless nativity on the coffee table by the loveseat. The air was fresh with the scent of garlands wound around the stair banister and evergreen centerpieces adorned with candles.

The pine scent mingled with the spicy scent of the simmering potpourris in the living room and den. Later, scents of fresh baked cookies, nut bread, and cinnamon rolls would lend a warm feeling to the air. The subtle aromas of chocolates, mints and hard candies lingered by dishes set here and there about the house. Oh, I know I shouldn't leave so much candy about. The child eats it by the handful. But Christmas, after all, is a time to celebrate bounty, isn't it?

The centerpiece of the house, of course, was the Christmas tree. We did have a bit of an argument that Saturday morning we picked it out. I chose a tree just a little taller than myself. It was the kind that had spaces between the boughs, a style I deemed best for displaying the ornaments. He chose a tree that must have been nine feet if it was an inch and as thick and bushy as they come. Well, he rather insisted and I decided that since we have so many ornaments, a taller tree would be a better choice.

How different last year was from this. The house was so barren and cold this year. Oh, I did put up the ornaments and Christmas collections as usual, but my heart was so empty and fearful. It was as if they weren't there at all.

But I am getting ahead of myself.

That Sunday night when the work was all done, my son sat in my lap, looking at the tree. The room was dark but for the fire in the fireplace and the flickering lights on the tree. Pinpoints of light, reflected from the ornaments on the walls, surrounded us like hundreds of fairy lights. The scent of our recently finished turkey dinner and fresh baked rolls whispered contentment. Crystalline harmonies of "God Rest Ye Merry Gentlemen" chimed from a shiny red music box.

'I love Christmas, Mummy,' he said to me. 'I especially love it when Santa Claus brings me lots of presents. I love new toys.'

'And I love you, my little man,' I said, hugging him close.

He looked up at me as if he had forgotten I was there. 'I love you too, Mummy. Now you can brush my teeth, tuck me in bed, and read me *three* stories.'

You see? He wasn't a spoiled child. Not really.

The next day, a crisp Monday morning more than a year ago, I took him to my mother's house as usual. 'Grammy' took care of him while I was busy with my society in town. That day we were to help the Minister with his bookkeeping and meet to plan the Christmas Pageant. Tuesday it would be tea and book buying with friends. Wednesday would be entirely taken settling the widow Flemming and her daughters in their former house having just returned from disappointment and failure on the Iowa plains. On Thursday my society would often have serious debates over lunch in the Thaddeus Lowrey Gardens. Friday would be spent shopping for household dry goods. So it went in countless variation, week after week.

Truth be told, I was afraid Mother would tire of caring for my child before he reached school age. He can be difficult at times. But my mother had such patience! I have known her to get him to bathe and, heaven be praised, take a nap. Once, if the story is to be believed, she got him to eat vegetables!

I felt such a cold humor in my chest when I heard of these things. Why couldn't he have been obedient under my care? I am convinced it would have precluded what happened earlier this Christmas season. If he had only had some appreciation of my love and efforts on his behalf, perhaps the horror and misery that occurred could have been avoided.

The bitter winter days arrived in anticipation of Christmas Day. Some days my child was insufferable. He just couldn't understand why it wasn't the Eve of Christmas 'tonight after dinner.' He insisted it would be and accused me of lying if I tried to convince him otherwise. If it hadn't been for the mister's traditions giving us occasions to look forward to, I don't know what I would have done.

The day of the family daguerreotype came. We dressed in the matching clothes Grammy made us: a long dress for me in cheery red, green and black plaid and a matching blazer and tie for my little man. The blazer went well with the little red vest and black pants I bought for him in town. Mother made bows for herself and attached them to a hat and blouse that she already owned. She said the plaid bows made her look 'part of the little family.'

The sleigh ride to fetch Grammy and go into town, I am proud to relate, went without a tantrum of any kind. We only had a little trouble at the photography parlor keeping the child still. But when the photographer called for the poses to be held, he put on the most adorable stoic look. I knew the resulting photograph would be outstanding, and it was. The day was a success.

I wish I could say the same about our visit with Santa Claus. I will admit it was my fault for neglecting to pull Santa aside and warn him.

On the day Santa was to make his annual visit to our village square, I had a particularly hard time convincing the child to wear his matching outfit. He said the collar was 'too scratchy.' Well, it hadn't been too scratchy the first time he wore it! After much argument, I finally had to insist. He wouldn't hear any of it so I had to sit on him and dress his wiggling self. Afterwards he tore the tie and threw off the blazer. I grabbed him before he could jump on them.

'Is this how you behave on the day we are to see Santa Claus?' I said. 'You know he brings ill-behaved children coal and coal alone. What shall I tell him when we see him today in the village square?'

He stopped his struggling and looked at me. Jerking his arm free of my grasp, he quickly picked up the blazer and ruined tie and ran to his room. In a few moments he reappeared wearing the blazer. It appeared that he had tried to comb his hair. It stuck out on one side.

'I look handsome without a tie, don't I Mummy?' he said, beaming as if nothing had happened. 'Santa never wears a tie himself and I don't believe he expects the children who see him to wear one, do you?'

I laughed in spite of myself. 'I expect not.'

Again we rode to Grammy's house on the way to the village. She remarked on the absent tie and the child explained how his mother and he had decided against wearing it that day.

My mother gave me a knowing look. I pretended not to see.

The three of us arrived in the town square in high spirits having sung our favorite Christmas carols on the last leg of the drive. There he was! Jolly Santa Claus sitting in the carved wooden throne. The Mayor's wife, Mrs. Morrison was at his right hand, dressed in red and white velvet with white ermine trim matching her muff and bonnet. Santa was speaking in the most animated way with the boy on his lap who constantly giggled and hid his eyes. The boy's parents admonished him for being so shy with Santa.

Two sisters and their parents waited on Santa's left. The father held the youngest girl in his arms. A chilly emptiness spread through my heart as I looked on the two families. How I missed my son's father. Had he survived the consumption, my child would have had a strong hand to guide him to adulthood.

My child, of course, wanted to walk right up and sit on Santa's lap. After a small tug-of-war and a whispered discussion of how Santa values patience in a child, he was willing to wait on line. This would have been the time to approach Santa with a quiet word to use caution in what he said to the child. But how could I have known what was about to happen?

In a short while my child was on Santa's lap expounding on each and every toy he expected for Christmas. How proud I was of his memory, to remember all the toys on his long list. How wide did Santa's eyes grow as the long list grew longer. This, too, should have given me warning to intervene. But too late!

Santa interrupted the child in mid sentence. 'Ho, ho, ho, ho-o-o-o! Perhaps a child who was good as gold would receive half of these treasures. Yet by all reports you are far from pure.'

He paused to look at my child, who was slowly turning beet red. 'All or nothing!' my child yelled at the top of his lungs.

'Ah well,' Santa's voice became gruff, 'nothing then. Nothing but coal for a spoiled child like you!'

With that my child did smack Santa on the nose with the flat of his hand. Santa held his nose and stood suddenly, dumping the child on the ground. My mother looked as if she would faint. Mrs. Morrison peeped an 'OH!' and looked at me with alarmed eyes. I rushed to grab the child before he could kick Santa in the knee. I pulled the wiggling boy to our sleigh, collecting Mother with my free arm along the way.

Oh the humiliation! This story would spread through the village in less than an afternoon. I was so angry I clenched my teeth and sat in heated silence the entire way home. Mother fanned herself with her gloves, staring at the child.

'Child, do you realize what you've done?' she asked. 'Because you lack the ability to check your anger, you have ruined your own Christmas.'

The boy had been sitting with his arms clenched tightly at his chest until he heard this. Surprise spread across his face. He looked at me, but I was too angry to return his gaze.

'But it was his own fault," he said.

'You just keep saying that to yourself as you sit in a room devoid of toys on Christmas morning,' Grammy said.

◞◟

'Is it true?' the child asked tearfully. We were now at home having left my Mother off at her house. 'What Grammy said? Will Santa pass by our house on Christmas Eve?'

'Perhaps,' I said.

The child wrinkled his brow in thought. 'Mummy, help me write a note to Santa. I'll say I'm sorry. I'll ask him to forgive me.'

We spent the hour after dinner at my writing desk composing a letter on my best parchment. The child drew a picture of our house at the bottom and wrote 'don't forget to stop here' in his own hand. I sealed the envelope with a drop of red wax.

'Now Santa will not be mad at me any more,' he said and kissed the cooled wax. 'Now he will bring me all the toys.'

'Perhaps,' I said quietly.

◞◟

Christmas Day came. Joy of joys! And surprise of all surprises, the living room was filled with brightly wrapped presents. Boxes with bows were piled in stacks around the Christmas tree.

The child was a blur of activity. Squealing with happiness and wonder as he flew into the mountain of presents. Frantically tearing open gift after gift. Glancing briefly at each in turn. Throwing toy after toy aside to grab the next. Discarded wrapping paper reached knee-high.

The merriment was accompanied by Mother's victrola playing brass choir carols. The scent of warm honey cakes wafted from the kitchen. Candles flickered with the child's rush from one side of the room to another.

Kicking the new ball through the door to the den while wearing the outlandish purple mask with the long nose. Sailing the tiny warships across the coffee table and letting them 'fall off the edge of the world.' Riding the stick pony at break-neck speed through every room, screaming like an attacking Indian all the while. Staging a duel between the stuffed bunny and the new teddy bear. The child didn't stop running and jumping for two solid hours!

I ran after him picking up toys and occasionally admonishing him for being too rough on his new playthings.

Then it was time for a quick breakfast of the cooled honey cakes and coffee with lots of cream. Between mouthfuls, my child told me which toys Santa neglected to bring, but that it didn't matter because he got most of the things he really wanted.

So you see my child could not have been called 'spoiled.'

At least, I didn't think so until the events of this year's Christmas Season began to unfold.

CHAPTER 2
Abduction of the Child

Thanksgiving dinner went well this year. The meal I prepared was well received by my mother and our special guest, my child's primary teacher. My mother brought pumpkin pie and the schoolmarm brought … a book on child discipline.

I had invited the teacher, Miss Schleswig as an act of atonement. Although I didn't show it, the presentation of the book offended me greatly. It is true my child's first three months in public school were difficult on us all, but giving me such a book was presumptuous to say the least! After that disastrous first week in September I began looking for a private boy's school. The nearest one was twenty miles away and very expensive. There was really no practical alternative to our local two-room schoolhouse.

As I said, the dinner went well. I don't think Miss Schleswig saw the child spit his green beans on the floor. I dropped my fork and did a quick clean-up with my napkin. The child did eat his turkey but would touch nothing else. Threats of 'no desert' had no effect.

After dinner we retired to the living room. Mother put a shovel full of chestnuts on the fire and they began to sputter and pop as I served the hot spiced cider. The aroma set me to mind of the coming Christmas season.

The conversation turned to the village school. I had attended the same school as a child although it was but one room at that time. Master Pinchall was still there, now in the capacity of secondary master and school principal. Mr. Pinchall, whose penetrating, narrow-eyed stare through rimless glasses had not lessened in the twenty years since my first class with him at age six.

It was Master Pinchall who considered expelling my child after the cutting of Jennifer McLinn's long braided hair. Expulsion! As if my child was intentionally evil or destructive. I still maintain that Miss Schleswig was at fault in this. If she just had passed out the paper first, before the scissors, there would have been no problem. After all, what did she expect my child to do with scissors in one hand and Jennifer McLinn's left braid draped across the other?

I am thankful Miss Schleswig did not bring this matter up during the course of the evening's conversation. She did, however, page through the book she had brought, point out the most salient chapters. 'Spare the Switch and Spoil the Child', indeed! This book would find the way to the bottom of my linen drawer the very moment the schoolmarm stepped out the door.

The day after Thanksgiving arrived with as crisp and cold a morning as you could want. Decorating day was here! I should have been lighthearted and happy, but I wasn't. The beautiful Christmas ornaments that had always brought cheer and anticipation of the coming Holidays did not have the same effect on me this year.

Why was my child more difficult than ever to control? He insisted on hanging wreaths himself even though he was not nearly nimble enough for the task. He became frustrated and ruined one of my most treasured wreaths before I could stop him. I dragged him to his room, struggling and shrieking, and on arrival, he bit me on the arm.

One would think the child would regret his actions having heard his mother scream, but no. He pounded on his door as usual, screaming to be let out. I could not bear to switch him, no matter what Miss Schleswig's book recommended, though I was indeed tempted after this latest tantrum.

The next day was less productive. The child decided for some unknown reason we should have two Christmas trees this year: one in the living room and one in the dining room. No argument would change his thought. I was unable to lessen his resolve no matter how I tried. I gave up, thinking that when the time came, he would listen to reason.

We drove the carriage to the west forest to see the woodsman who supplied us annually with the most perfect trees. The chill in the air was particularly biting this morning. Fortunately, the woodsman's cottage was not far into the wood.

The cottage stood in a clearing dominated by an irregular rocky slope. Nine trees stood in wooden buckets on the shady side of the woodsman's home. The woodsman, a stocky stump of a man, heard the bells on our horse's harness and came out the rustic front door to greet us.

My child jumped out of the carriage before it stopped completely. He was running in and around the trees by the time I joined him. The smallest tree was knocked over in his excitement.

'We don't want that one anyway, Mummy,' he said as I righted the tree.

'These two!' he shouted, pointing out the two largest ones. 'This one for the living room and this one for the dining room. And look! Here is one that will be perfect for the drawing room. Three trees! We shall have three trees this year!'

I groaned inwardly. He was so exuberant I found it hard to contradict his ideas.

'There is only room in the carriage for one tree,' I said. 'How could we possibly consider three?'

'But you promised we could have two trees!' he shouted. 'You PROMISED!'

I know I had never promised any such thing, but to say so would only throw the child into a fit. I turned and asked the woodsman if he had rope to bind two trees into the carriage.

The other traditions that we usually looked forward to in the days and weeks ahead were not observed this year. They were cast aside by the horrible event I am about to recount for you.

⌣

It was the evening of December 5th, St. Nicholas Eve. The child had just thrown a fit because I told him the collection of cast metal sailors and pirates that he wanted for Christmas were no longer in the village toy store. Mrs. Halverson had purchased them for her grandson.

'You're lying to me! They're still there, and if they weren't Santa could bring them to me anyway. I want them. I want them, and I'll have them on Christmas morning or I'll find Santa and bite him. I'll bite you both!'

As usual, he had to be dragged to his room where he commenced kicking and beating the door. He was screeching at the top of his lungs about how he hated living here with me.

Suddenly, the din stopped. I heard him talking. Then I heard nothing. Silence. I walked to his room with a feeling of dread in the pit of my stomach. I opened the door slowly, hoping to see him asleep on his bed. Instead, I faced an empty room. Toys and clothes on the floor, window closed and latched, no child.

I frantically looked under the bed and in the wardrobe, calling him to come out from wherever he was hiding. I ran to the window, unlatched and threw it open. I leaned out calling his name in all directions. He wouldn't have run away in this cold weather, would he?

The silence gave me to know he was gone from the house. I turned from the window and rushed to the door. That is when I saw it: the switch.

'Switch? No it's just a stick,' I told myself. 'The boy is always playing with sticks.'

Even as I formed these words in my mind, I knew they were wrong. I didn't know how I knew, but it couldn't be anything else but a switch.

It was lying in the middle of the floor. I picked it up. It sparkled as I moved it in the light. Frost and ice crystals gleamed from tiny crevasses in the wood. In spite of the fact it was cold as an icecicle, I clutched it to my breast as I looked one more time about the room.

I rushed through the house calling my child's name. My little boy was gone! Disappeared! Stolen! Yes, that was it. There can be no other explanation for his disappearance.

I clutched the switch as I hurriedly put on my greatcoat and lit a lantern. I tore open the front door and ran out into the night. Mrs. Hargrove's husband saw me searching the child's favorite hiding places, calling his name. He dropped the armload of firewood he had been carrying into his house and ran to my aid. Searching the area produced nothing. Mr. Hargrove harnessed his horse and he and his wife drove me to the nearest neighbors and from there to the village constable's house. We roused him from his hearth to accompany us back to my house to investigate. Search as he might, Constable Wickerson could find no clue as to what happened to my boy. He questioned me in great detail: what events led up to the boy's disappearance, if he had ever run away from home, what he was wearing, who his playmates were, who may have harbored a grudge against me or my late husband. He wanted to know everything I said, everything I saw, everything I heard. Everything was said twice, three times.

Then there was nothing else to say or do. There should have been something more to do. Something we hadn't thought of, but there wasn't. He was gone and words were not bringing him back.

Finally, Constable Wickerson said, 'I'll return in the morning with my deputies and their dogs. If he's outside, he'll be uncomfortable, but I don't think he'll be in danger of exposure. Try and get some sleep. You will need your energy tomorrow.'

Mrs. Hargrove offered to stay the night with me. I could barely murmur 'no, I'll be all right.'

All right was something I would never be again.

∿

Home, cold home.

Rest? Sleep? I could do neither.

Lying on my back in my dreary bed, I clutched the switch to the bodice of my nightclothes. My heart pounded as if I had been running. Fears of every description tore through my mind. What was happening to my child right now at this moment? Where was he? Was he in pain?

How could I have stopped this from happening?

My heart pounded and the switch, held tight to my breast, vibrated.

Where was he? Where?

What horrible fear was he feeling right now?

What?

The switch trembled with the beat of my heart. It quivered.

If only I was omniscient. If only I could fly to his side.

Oh, please dear Lord, let him not be hurt.

I cried. I hurt deep within my body and mind.

My heart hammered a quick, uneven rhythm and the switch vibrated in sympathy. Its vibration created an inaudible drone that hummed at the edges of my thoughts. The clock began to strike midnight and the switch murmured in counterpoint.

The drone of the switch wove through the sound of the chimes, gaining in insistence. I was so deeply immersed in my sorrow, I didn't notice.

The clock struck twelve! My mind's tension snapped, propelling me into the depths of the drone that had enveloped me. I flew, I floated, I hovered. Grey pain cleared from my eyes and I looked down on my child's room.

He was there! He was kicking and striking the door. He was yelling at the top of his lungs.

Those sounds! Those familiar sounds. They were the very sounds I had heard earlier this very evening, though it seemed years ago.

'Let me out! Don't leave me in here! I hate you. You're so mean to me. I want to get out of here forever! I'll go away to a new family!'

A movement caught the edge of my vision. A flutter. Then a man stepped from the shadow by the curtain. How had he gotten into our house? He was a tall gaunt man dressed in black, a long black cape draped casually over one shoulder. On his handsome face he wore a full black beard streaked with silver. He carried an open book in one hand and had a sack of switches on his back. On his right arm and right leg was wound the most beautiful golden chain, the ends of which trailed down to the floor and terminated in a golden, jewel-encrusted box.

'You, child, will come with me,' he said and closed the book with a whack.

His voice was deep but not resonant. Rather, it was cold and hollow. His presence caused the senses to come to anxious awareness as if it were a predator that stalked the room. He advanced a step, dragging the chains and box.

'Come!'

My child sank down onto the floor, trembling. He looked so small and frightened, but his voice was still defiant. 'Who are you and what are you doing in my room? I'm not going anywhere with you! Mummy!'

'My name is Black Peter, although I am known as "Krampus" by many. You have much to fear from me. Hope is not lost to you, however, for I am kept at bay.'

His handsome face then did curl into an ugly sneer and he said, 'Kept at bay by St. Nicholas himself. He has bound me to his purpose with these chains,' Black Peter shook his fist making the chains jingle like glass bells, 'and a tiny fleck of his spirit.' The gaunt man's gesture indicated the jeweled box on the floor by his right foot. 'I do his bidding every St. Nicholas Eve; then only!'

He bent over to pick up my little boy. As he did, a switch fell out of his pack. He looked down at the switch and then turned his face up. His cold eyes met mine. I was frozen. Hypnotized as a bird entranced by a snake.

As I looked into his eyes, he began to fade. With my boy in his arms he began to fade. Fade. Gone.

I was back in myself. Back in bed.

'NO-O-O-O!' I screamed. 'A nightmare to torture me. That's what it was. A false vision meant to tear my heart; to intensify my horrible solitude.'

The clock began to strike the hour. With each chime, the sparkling switch in my hands trembled more violently. One, two, three, four, five, six, seven, eight, nine, ten, eleven…

Chapter 3
Spirited Away

... Twelve! I was hurled from my body into a weightless silence. A gray purgatory swirled around me bringing with the sense of sound alone. The whistle of a cold wind was heard but not felt. The rhythms of distant voices crept about me like raindrops in mist. Two voices began to be more prominent within the whispers of many. The voices approached. Rhythms and sounds crystallized into words.

'Where is my room? Put me down! You can't take me without my mummy's permission. Put me down!' It was the voice of my child! His tone became more insistent and demanding with each sentence.

I saw them then: Black Peter taking slow, measured strides, my child struggling weakly in his arms. The multi-tonal gray surrounding them did not swirl with their passing as might a fog. Rather, it gave the impression of solid mass seeping with images of wraiths. Images that were in motion.

I had never experienced or even imagined the look of this before. My presence looked on unblinking and then weightlessly followed their progress. Black Peter carried my child without thought to his comfort. The man's features were distant and emotionless. I could not bear the horror of watching my child kidnapped before my eyes, but was helpless to look away.

Black Peter spoke. It wasn't clear to me whether he meant to address the child or merely to fill the gray void with sound. 'In an unguarded moment nearly five hundred years ago, St. Nicholas captured me and bound me in the chains of his spirit. I must do his bidding from sunset on December 5th to sunrise on St. Nicholas Day, December 6th.'

He looked down at the child as if this should be important to him. The child only squirmed and tried to kick free of Peter's grip.

'The task demanded of me by Nicholas is to collect spoiled, belligerent children and spirit them away.'

My child stopped kicking. He stared into Black Peter's face. He slowly looked around him. He looked in the direction of my presence, but did not see me.

'The *children?*' he shouted. 'There aren't any other children. I am the only one. And I am *not* spoiled. You can't call me that. You don't even know me.'

'You think you are the only one?' He gave forth a mocking laugh. 'There are many, and I am with each one as we speak. BEHOLD!'

As he spoke the last word, Black Peter tossed his head causing the horns jutting through his hood to slash the void. The variegated gray rippled all around them and then became clear in all directions. There appeared a march of hundreds of Black Peters carrying innumerable kicking, screaming, begging, crying children. Each of the Black Peters was identical but the children in their arms were all different. Pleas in a dozen different languages could be heard simpering through the crystal surroundings.

With a nod of his head, ripples of gray spread from the points of his horns occluding the scene as suddenly as it had appeared. Black Peter's measured stride had not slowed.

The child began to struggle again. 'Put me down! I'm not one of them. Those were brats. Stupid, noisy brats! Where do you think you are taking me?' the child's voice became a shriek. 'My mother will take you to task for this!'

17

'Your mother knows of your plight and is helpless to intervene,' Black Peter said as he glanced in my direction. 'She will know of your new home. She will see you in the lap of your new family and know that you are not being mistreated. Such is the command of Nicholas.'

'New family? … New home? What do you mean? I'm not going to any new home. I have a home. You take me back there this instant.'

Black Peter laughed a chilling laugh as the faded into the ragged solidity of the gray void.

∽

The salty smell of the sea permeated the gray as whispers and cries marched into silence. The cries of children were replaced by the distant roar of waves breaking on a rocky shore. Then came a rage of wind carrying the scent of pine and frozen earth. The gale grew to frightening strength and the sounds of trees thrashing and breaking tore through the gray void. With a great rush of sound, the gray was hurled away revealing a scene etched in razor sharp morning colors.

Sea cliffs surrounding a shallow bay descended like great white steps to a shabby fishing village on the far shore. Fishing boats floundered at anchor in the fierce winds. Grey clouds were driven across the dismal sky by the unbearably cold wind.

I knew the cold but could not feel it. I hovered above a clearing near the rim of the highest cliff. At the north edge of the barren ground, a rude cabin squatted amidst pines thrashing and creaking in the gale. The cottage was very roughly made and seemed to list to one side. It had a turf roof, oilskin windows, and a chimney loosely constructed of riverbed rocks and clay. The cabin had a rickety porch on the side that overlooked the bay. There on the porch, curled in a ball and shivering uncontrollably, sat my child.

Where was Black Peter? Had he just deposited the child here and left? I looked at the horizon and saw the morning sun send cold morning rays over the distant round-shouldered mountains.

'Ah,' I thought, 'his duty to St. Nicholas ends at sunrise. So now my child is abandoned here in the cold.'

I wished for a voice to shout to my child to go knock on the door of the cabin. I had none. The gale howled with a mocking sound. My child looked over his shoulder at the front door.

Just then a sharp gust of wind tore a huge branch from a nearby tree, throwing it on the roof of the porch with a crash. Before the branch had turned over and fallen to the ground, my child had sprung up, run to the door, flung it open and run in. The wind slammed the door behind him.

My presence advanced slowly on the cabin. Oh how I wished I could control my movements. It was agonizing to move so slowly when I knew my child was in a strange place without me. I approached the door and winced as I passed through the wood panel as if it was insubstantial as smoke.

Inside, the scene was frozen in time. A man and woman and two girls all dressed in shabby, patched clothing stood by the fire in a wide stone hearth. They stared at my child. He stared back. My child broke the silence.

'What are you looking at?' he said.

'You burst into our house without so much as a knock and ask what *we* are looking at?' the man growled.

'I had to come in! The wind is tearing down trees.'

'Who are you? You are not of the village. How did you get all the way out here in those clothes without freezing to death?'

'I wouldn't have come in this ugly house if I didn't have to!' my child said loudly. I cringed, hoping they wouldn't mistake his frightened tone for disrespect. 'You can't make me go out there again,' he shrieked. 'You can't!'

The man made a growling noise deep in his chest. 'No one comes in my own house uninvited and gives me affront. Child or no, you are going out the way you came in.'

The man stepped forward, opened the door and shoved the child out. If the man had been a second slower with his push, the child would have bitten him on the arm. I saw his teeth flash as he went out.

'Father!' said the woman, standing up quickly. The man ignored her and latched the door. 'Carl, how could you?'

'I would have allowed him to stay a while and warm himself...' The door suddenly thumped with kicking and banging from outside. '... but we couldn't afford to feed him in any case,' he finished through clenched teeth.

'Let me in,' could be heard amid the rattling thumps and howling of the wind.

Carl's face darkened. He turned abruptly and took a step toward the door. The woman rushed to put herself between him and the door. There was fear in her eyes.

'Out of my way, Mother. He should be taught a lesson.'

The girls ran to one of the rough sleeping pallets and jumped on top, hugging each other. The man glanced back at them and hesitated.

'Don't go out, Father,' the woman said. 'Let me talk to him.'

'No. No one will go out,' the man gritted. 'The cold can have him. He will either survive on his own or not. It doesn't matter to us.'

I couldn't believe my ears. This man was fully prepared to let my child die of exposure!

The woman would have said more, but the pounding on the door stopped suddenly and everyone tuned to look at it. The woman unlatched the door and peeked out a crack.

My mind panicked. What was she seeing? Had my child passed out from the cold? Had the roof of the porch collapsed on him? Oh, something terrible has happened, I know it! Open the door. I cannot move my presence of my own accord.

'He is walking away,' the woman said. 'Let me stop him, Father. 'The village is too far for such a small one. And in the weather…'

'No, Mother,' the man said stonily. 'We must let him go and forget he was ever here. We don't have resources enough for our own children, let alone an offensive stranger child.'

'How dare he?' my mind seethed. 'How could he be so heartless? Surely he could spare a warm meal. No one is that poor. And was he too busy to help the child find his way home?'

Just then there came a quiet knock on the door. The woman glanced at her husband and opened the door. There stood my child, lips blue and teeth chattering. His shivering jerked his small body with shuddering jolts.

'May I come in? It is very cold out here and I have nowhere to go.'

The woman shot an icy glance at the man, picked up my boy and carried him to the fire. She wrapped him in a tattered comforter and sat on a rocking chair with him on her lap.

The man stepped close to the hearth, towering over my child. 'How did you come here, child?'

The child still chattered, but he answered politely enough. 'I was taken from my room in the night and brought here by Black Peter.'

'Black Peter?' the man scowled. 'Did he say he was known by other names? "Hans Trapp" or "Krampus"?'

'Yes!' said the child. 'He said he was known as "Krampus" by many.'

The girls gasped and the woman put her hand to her mouth. They stared at the child with wide eyes. The man gave a quiet groan and looked down with his arms folded tightly across his chest.

'You have been touched by the devil himself, child,' said the man. 'Do you know the legend of Krampus and his task on the night of St. Nicholas Eve?'

My child wiggled deeper into the folds of the comforter. 'He… he said he was directed by St. Nicholas to collect children…'

'*Spoiled* children,' the man interrupted. 'Ill-mannered and belligerent children are collected and spirited away. Spirited away to places unknown.' He looked at the child with piercing eyes. 'Until now.'

'It seems Krampus has set you on our doorstep expecting us to take you in.' The man turned away. 'What a cruel trick he has played on us. If we do take you in we will all be in dire straights before winter breaks. We do not have stores enough to last us the season even without another mouth to feed. Perhaps there is a family in town who could…'

'Father,' the woman said, 'I can't believe St. Nicholas would direct Krampus to do something that would destroy our family. Perhaps if you teach him the trade he could help you at sea. We would have greater profit this season.'

The man looked up. 'Of course. St. Nicholas has caused a boy-child to be delivered to us to learn my trade. A boy who will grow to manhood and support us in our old age.'

'I won't *be* here in your old age. I won't! I'm going to walk home as soon as can be. It can't be far. Black Peter carried me for only a short while.'

The man gave a derisive snort. 'Your home is most likely hundreds of miles distant. It wouldn't be like Krampus to allow an easy escape from his devilry.

'No, child. You will remain with us until death.'

I could bear no more. My heart was broken. My child was gone. Separated from me forever. A chill clutched my heart. He was sentenced to a life of poverty with a heartless family. Destined to scratch out a meager existence until the day he dies.

The scene dissolved into troubled thoughts. Was I such a poor mother that I should be punished in such a horrible manner? How could I have given him more of my time, my income, myself?

I opened my eyes to a cold bedroom. My bedroom. The switch I clutched with both hands no longer sparkled with frost.

The clock! Was it about to strike twelve again? It must! I must be carried back to my child's side. To comfort him. To find comfort myself.

My eyes snapped to the place where my clock sat on the dresser drawers. The face was visible in the light of dawn. Six o'clock.

I faced a new day alone. Perhaps a new life.

Alone.

Chapter 4
The Poor Family

My name is Frieda, but I have been called 'Mother' for so long I answer more readily to that. My husband, Carl, is also comfortable with his family title of 'Father.' My daughters are Elsa, seven years old, and Bretta, nine. And then there is Jonathan. Or perhaps I should say 'was' though it breaks my heart.

He came to us on St. Nicholas morn, tossed on our doorstep by Krampus himself. We were sitting by the fire saying prayers for the day. The weather was so cold outside we continued to feed the fire after breakfast. All of a sudden the boy burst through our front door. A chill followed him. A chill that seemed to watch the events silently. It was an unsettling feeling that I have not experienced before or since.

We were stunned by his sudden appearance. Even more so when we heard his story.

Father, gruff bear that he is, threw little Jonathan out into the cold. But it was not so easy to undo such unholy mischief. Jonathan returned in such a pitiable state! Not even Carl's stern heart could deny him.

Elsa liked Jonathan from the beginning. She was not afraid of him even though she knew he had been touched by Krampus. Nor was she put off by his strident behavior. Bretta tolerated him warily and, in the end, cared for him a great deal.

While I sat with him on my lap that St. Nicholas morning, Elsa came right up and took his cold hand in hers. He pulled away, but she insisted.

'My name is Elsa,' she said. 'I haven't ever had a boy friend before. Now we three can be friends and play house together. You and Bretta can be father and mother and Brunda and I can be the children.'

Elsa tucked her doll, Brunda, under Jonathan's arm. Brunda was her treasure, her only play toy. Father had carved and painted the wooden face and I had made the yarn hair and fabric body stuffed with dried moss. Brunda's arm had recently come off, but Elsa played with her just the same. She understood that we were out of thread and would have to wait for income from the next catch to buy more.

Jonathan looked down at the doll. He was mortified. 'Boy friend?! Play house?… with girls and a broken doll? I don't play with dolls and I don't play with girls.'

He threw Brunda down on the floor. Elsa yelped, picked her up and cradled her like a hurt child. Bretta leveled a poisonous look at Jonathan.

'I play with sailors and ships,' he continued, ignoring Bretta.

Father's eyebrows went up. 'You have an interest in the sea, child?'

'Yes,' said Jonathan, his mood changing in an instant. 'Men of the sea are strong and courageous. They have many adventures and are always victorious.'

Father drew himself up very straight and smiled his hard half smile. 'I am a fisherman by trade. I own my own dory and cast nets. I mostly bring up scup, ocean perch and haddock, but…'

'Fish!' shouted Jonathan. 'I thought I smelled the stink of fish in here. BLAHhhhhh! I *hate* fish. No one can make me eat it! Not even Grammy.'

Father's face turned to stone. 'You may well starve to death then. Fish is all we have. That, a sack of potatoes and a sack of onions. And precious little of each.'

'I'll starve then,' said the boy turning up his nose. 'I don't need food anyway.'

The girls looked at each other. 'Starve' was not a word to be used lightly. Last winter had been so harsh we had been unable to venture out most of January. Father had been unable to fish because of the ice floe that developed in December. Our supply of smoked fish had run out completely and we were down to one end of moldy bread when the thaw came. We had kept our bellies near empty for over a month. Oh, yes, the word 'starve' had real meaning to the four of us.

I was still apprehensive three hours later while I prepared the midday meal. I decided on the fish stew atop stale bread. It was one of the girls favorites and I hoped Jonathan would receive it well for his sake. With this thought I glanced at Carl rocking by the fire, smoking his pipe and sharpening his gaffe.

The girls helped by slicing the bread and setting the table. We only had four spoons, but I told them I would make due with a knife. Bretta had brought out our special tablecloth, the one I had crocheted while heavy with her. I was surprised that Bretta considered this such an important occasion.

Jonathan had fallen asleep on the hearth, still wrapped in the comforter. Father glanced at him occasionally and then pulled the stone all the harder across the gaffe point.

Finally the stew was ready. Elsa ran to the fireside. 'The meal is ready, Father.' Kneeling down by Jonathan, she took his hand and said, 'Wake up, sleepyhead. You must be hungry by now.'

Jonathan sat up and rubbed his eyes. 'I am. What is it?' He stood, letting the comforter slide to the floor. He wrinkled his nose. 'I don't like the smell of it.'

'You'll like it,' Bretta said. 'It'll warm you right to your toes.'

Elsa led the men to the table, Father in one hand and Jonathan in the other. Carl's eyebrows raised at the sight of the tablecloth but he said nothing.

When all were seated, Father said Grace while Jonathan sniffed the pot. Bretta served the bread slices and I followed her with the stew. As I approached Jonathan, he stood on the chair and warded me off with both hands.

'No! Don't slop that goo on my bread. Just give me some butter.'

Father set his spoon down with a bump. Storm clouds could not have looked more threatening. 'We have no butter. *This* is what we have,' he said nodding at his plate. 'We may have butter on St. Lucia's day if I have success at sea and market. In the meantime, accept what is given you and be thankful.'

I glanced from Carl to Jonathan and then back to Carl. He nodded. I put a ladle full of stew on Jonathan's bread.

'NO!' screamed the child pushing the plate away so hard it overturned on my precious tablecloth. He picked up his spoon and threw it at me. 'Get me something else. Get it now!'

Father stood, glaring at the child. He towered over the table trembling with anger. His big callused hands were clenched into fists. I had never seen him so angry.

Jonathan saw his expression and was afraid. He tried to crawl under the table but Father caught him by the belt and lifted him like baggage.

'Father!' I cried. 'He's but a child…'

Carl stalked to the door oblivious to everything about him. He wrenched open the door and stormed out, the boy suspended by his side.

'Coats!' I said to his retreating back. 'The wind is calmed but still frigid.'

Carl backhanded the door with his free hand, slamming it in my face. I quickly picked up the comforter from the hearth, wrapped it around me and went outside to watch from the porch. I made the girls stay inside but they still peeked through a crack in the door.

Father carried Jonathan to the edge of the wood and dropped him. Carl's husky voice carried all the way to where I stood.

'First find a warren that is unoccupied. Bear, fox, or badger. Your body heat will keep you through the night. Only come out to find food.' Father bent and pulled up a handful of stiff grass. 'This will only fill your belly. Don't depend on it or you will starve.'

Carl walked to a withered shrub and dug at its foot with his knife. He uncovered a lumpy white root, cut it free and threw it on the ground. 'This will sustain you for a while, but to make it through winter alive, you will need to eat flesh. You are not skilled enough to catch birds or small animals, so this is your only recourse,' he said pointing at a rock embedded in the cold earth. Father bent and with a groan, pulled the rock free. The bottom of the hole wiggled with fat, worm-like insect larvae. Carl dug out a handful and held the squirming mass in front of Jonathan's startled face.

'The first time, swallow them without chewing. They're not as good as fish, but when you are starving you won't mind.' Father dropped the writhing insects, turned and walked toward me. I saw Jonathan stand and stare at the grubs, both hands covering his mouth. He gagged. He looked at Father and back to the pile of larvae.

Jonathan broke into a run, caught up with Father and grabbed him about the leg. 'Don't leave me out here with the bugs. I'm sorry. I'm so sorry. I won't be able to live out here alone. I'll die.'

Jonathan slid down to Father's foot and Father had to stop.

'I promise not to do anything to make you mad. I won't eat your food. I'll sleep on the floor. I won't talk to anybody. You won't even know I'm there.'

Father looked down disapprovingly and then looked at me. I nodded encouragingly. Father stooped, picked up Jonathan by the belt and strode to where I was standing on the porch. Without slowing or looking anywhere but straight ahead, he dropped Jonathan at my feet and continued on into the house.

〜

The first day passed. Jonathan hid behind a sleeping palate during dinner. That night he slept on the floor, even though Bretta and Elsa made room for him on their straw mattress. All the next day he sat in a corner, watching us go about our work. Elsa put a cup of water by him and he would drink when he thought no one was watching. However he would hide during meals and ignore invitations to join us. When dinner was served on his second full day of fasting, I could hear his stomach growling from where I sat at table.

Father exhaled noisily. He set his spoon down, stood and walked to where Jonathan was hiding. 'Come out and eat. I won't have you dying of starvation in my home. You will stink worse than fish.'

Jonathan snorted, trying to stifle his laughter, but he wouldn't come out. Father crawled over the straw mattress on the palate, reached behind, and hauled him out by the belt.

Father carried him to the table saying, 'This is a habit I would be glad to break. I should dump you in the soup instead of pouring the soup into you.'

Elsa, Bretta and I laughed. I hadn't heard banter like this out of Carl since he had courted me. Jonathan, however, sat at table with his head bowed. Elsa smoothed his hair and said, 'It's only broth and dried fish, but you should try. Here.' She handed him the steaming wooden mug.

His hands shook as he first sipped and then gulped the broth. He looked up. 'That's the best thing I ever tasted. Better than turkey.'

'Try the dried fish, Jonathan,' Bretta said, pushing over a thin piece the length of his hand. I glanced nervously at Carl. He seemed to be completely occupied by spooning more soup into his bowl.

Jonathan picked up the fish, sniffed it, and tried his best not to grimace. He looked at Father and saw that he was not watching. Jonathan quickly took a bite, chewed, chewed, chewed, and swallowed. He couldn't stop a quick shudder from shaking his body. He made a face.

'How was it?' I asked.

Father looked up, his face unreadable. Jonathan squeezed his mouth into something that resembled a smile.

'Beats the heck out of worms,' he said.

Three days passed. Jonathan wouldn't eat much at one sitting, but he did eat. Father kept his distance and rarely talked to him. The girls tried to include him in their chores, but he used a variety of reasons to excuse himself from work. He might get splinters if he carried wood, sweeping and dusting makes him sneeze horribly, washing with soap of any sort causes his skin to break out in a terrible red rash, and so on.

Once when asked what he thought he could do, he answered, 'I'm good at putting up Christmas decorations. I wouldn't mind doing that. It would make this ugly house look better. Where do you store them? My mother keeps ours in the attic. Boxes and boxes!'

Without pause, Jonathan began to describe all of the wonderful collections and decorations. He went into great detail about which carols the music boxes played, which nutcrackers were decorated with gold leaf and which were merely painted, where the nativities were made, what kinds of candy were put in which glass dishes. My head began to spin trying to imagine it.

'Stop,' I said. 'We have none of these things. The dressings of the house will be handmade of pine boughs and such, but we always wait 'till St. Lucia's day, December 13th, to begin. That is tomorrow, so some materials may be gathered today.'

'Really, Mother?' Elsa said with excitement. 'May we start now?'

I nodded. Elsa squealed, Bretta clapped her hands, and they both grabbed Jonathan's hands and dragged him to the door. We didn't have coats for the children, so they wrapped themselves in blankets and ran out the door. Bretta took a hand axe from the porch and Elsa got a large basket. Off they went into the forest.

Father had gotten up early that morning to do some small repairs on his nets and make preparations for the next fishing trip. Having finished before sunrise, he set out on the long walk to the village. He told me he would be back by suppertime.

The children were back in the early afternoon carrying cut pine boughs, fir cones, winter flowers, and long grasses for bindings. They left their treasures on the porch and came in for a cups of hot water to drink.

When Father appeared late in the afternoon, he seemed more somber than usual. We had to badger him at the dinner table to find out what had put in such morose mood.

'Well, if you must know,' he said, not looking up from his plate, 'there was an argument in the village about the weather.'

Jonathan's mouth dropped open, his eyebrows shot up, and he barked a disbelieving laugh. Father looked up crossly and Jonathan fell silent.

'I'm sorry,' Jonathan said quietly. 'I just thought it funny that men would get so upset about the weather.'

'Jonathan,' I said, 'you must understand that weather, especially bad weather, is no laughing matter to a man of the sea. Accurately reading the signs of approaching tempests could mean the difference between life and death.'

Father looked sideways at the wall. 'There were several merchants in the village whom I hadn't met before today. One was a surly character who insisted a storm was brewing. It didn't matter that every man on the dock disagreed with him.'

'Then you should not be worried, Father,' said Bretta. 'The man just can't read the sky like you can. He's wrong and you're right and that's all there is to it.'

Father said nothing for minute while he looked at his plate. He shook his head slightly as if to clear it. 'The other merchants were much more personable. One in particular was very talkative and we sat together for a while. He presented me with something unasked. A little surprise that will remain secret until the time is right.'

The girls knew not to press Father on this in spite of their curiosity. I noticed him glancing at Jonathan throughout the meal. The conversation turned to tonight's activities, for it was St. Lucia's Eve after all.

'I have never heard of this saint's day,' Jonathan said.

'It's a tradition from Sweden, the homeland of Mother's parents,' Bretta said. 'It started long ago when...'

'Bretta!' Elsa said. 'Mother has to tell it.'

'Yes, Bretta, you'll have to wait until you have your own household full of children and a husband.'

Bretta blushed and said no more.

We finished the meal and the girls began to clear the table. To everyone's surprise, Jonathan jumped up to help. The girls and I glanced at each other surreptitiously, but said nothing. Father brewed a tea from herbs the girls had gathered and dried. The aroma filled our small home with a spicy warmth. I handed cut roots to the children that tasted of licorice when chewed. Bretta banked the fire and set wild nuts by the coals to roast. Elsa gathered blankets and arranged them by the fire.

All was ready. We gathered in a half circle at the hearth and I began.

'Many generations ago in Sweden, the land of my parents birth, there came a terrible famine. Men and women, children and the elderly suffered greatly. Many died.

'My grandmother's great-great grandparents lived in a small village on the coast of the Gulf of Bothnia. Folk and Inga Kjelsen were their names. Their five children lived with them in a small cottage by a sparse forest.

'It was nearly the ides of December. There had been no food to speak of for weeks. The family had taken to foraging in the wood and the countryside for anything that was even remotely edible: pine nuts, roots, even grasses. At length they resorted to eating grubs and insects.'

Jonathan looked down quickly with look of horror on his brow.

'Finally, winter stripped the land clean. There was nothing. The days approached the winter solstice in gnawing, plodding progression. The day came that normally marked the Celebration of Light, the festival that anticipated longer days after so many overlong, darkened nights.

'No one in the isolated little village thought about a celebration in the midst of their deprivation. No procession of candles and torches, no bonfire, no oil lamps that would normally have been put in every window, and especially… no feast.

'The longest night arrived. On the night traditionally illuminated by hundreds of lights, there was only darkness and despair. Many had lost loved ones to starvation.

'Folk and Inga's youngest child, Johannes, was so weak they doubted he would last the night.

'Then, in the pitch-black hours before dawn, there came a brilliant light on the horizon, illuminating the great clouds from below. It shone as if every light from every Celebration of Light through the ages had been compressed into a single point.

'Every inhabitant of the village and outlying countryside awoke. None could sleep in the light that streamed through every crack in their poor homes. The light approached and as it did, it grew in brilliance. As the radiance came closer, a figure became visible in the center of the light. It was a young girl with a candle-lit wreath upon her head.

'St. Lucia.

'She was carrying a tray of warm breads and a pitcher of hot drink. She went from house to house feeding all in need. The pitcher never emptied, the tray never became bare. She came to the Kjelsen home singing a glorious song. St. Lucia fed the children and Folk and Inga without pausing in her song. Her brilliant light engulfed the village as she visited the last few homes. Her song increased as did her radiance as she dipped her head in farewell and continued on north.

'The famine was broken. Health and happiness returned to the Northland village. Each year ever after, St. Lucia's Day has been celebrated by recreating her visit. The family's eldest girl-child dons a white gown and places a candle-lit wreath on her head. She wakes the household in early morn to a breakfast of Lussekatter and coffee. This tradition has always insured a bountiful Christmas season.

Early the next morning we were visited by 'St. Lucia.' We couldn't really have slept through all of Bretta's preparations, but we pretended sleep all the same. This was the first year she asked to do it all herself without help from me. She had been up for hours baking Lussekatter, the traditional bread of St. Lucia, and brewing coffee. For the first time our little cabin was filled with an aroma of which Jonathan wholly approved. He said later that it reminded him of home.

I opened my eyes a crack. There stood St. Lucia in the glow of her candle-lit wreath. In her hands she held a thin board heaped with steaming rolls and a pitcher of coffee. By her side was a helper dressed in white, holding a candle of her own. The two girls began the song 'Nar Juldagsmorgan Glimmar' (When Christmas Morning is Dawning) and proceeded forward to rouse us from our beds. Bretta was dressed in the same white robe I had worn in my youth. Elsa had stolen Father's only white shirt, rolled up the sleeves and donned it with reverence, as one might a holy gown. Father couldn't bring himself to be angry. She looked so proud next to her sister.

The 'Saints' led us to the table and we prepared to breakfast. Jonathan picked up a knife and looked about the table. I believe he was looking for the butter Father had mentioned days ago.

Father stiffened a little. 'The nets are in full repair and the weather promises to be tolerable if not favorable. I shall go fishing tomorrow and, with luck, will bring in a catch sufficient to sell at market. Pray the margin of profit is enough to allow the purchase of what we need.'

Jonathan avoided his eyes, picked up a roll and took a big bite. 'This is all I need,' he said around the mouthful. 'It's delicious.'

The girls laughed and the feast began. Jonathan was quiet throughout the meal. He sat in dark contrast to the rest of the family who were in grand spirits. He finished only the one roll and sat with his hands folded in his lap and his head bowed. His cup of coffee rested by his plate, untouched.

After breakfast, we cleared the furniture from the middle of the room. We all joined hands and danced as we sang 'Nu Ar Det Jul Igen' (Yultide Is Here Again). I had tried to teach Jonathan the words the previous night, but he barely opened his mouth. He seemed so sad.

Father served the last of the coffee and I handed Jonathan his untouched cup. Father raised his own cup and said, 'A bountiful and happy Yuletide season will be ours. God bless us.'

'God bless us,' we all said and drained our cups. All but Jonathan.

His head was bowed as he looked into his cup. Then he slowly looked around the single room in which we lived. His gaze rested on the old, coarse drapery hanging before the translucent oil-paper windows, on the two sleeping pallets heaped with straw and covered with 'blankets' made from pieces of old clothes, on the rough, hand-made table and chairs. He then examined each of us one at a time, eyeing our old, thread-bare and tattered clothing. Finally, his eyes rested on his own clothes. Clothes I had made him as a change from the attire in which he arrived.

He sipped from his cup and set it on the table. 'This has no cream in it,' he said quietly. 'My mother would never have served it to me without cream.'

He walked to the pallet he shared with Bretta and Elsa and crawled under the covers. 'Mother would never have let me live in a place like this. Or clothed me in rags as you have.

'You have no bounty and never shall.'

CHAPTER 5
Storm At Sea

It was pitch black when Jonathan opened his eyes a crack. Black but for a single candle. Father's face hung like a flickering yellow specter in the darkness. His expression held a stern amusement.

'I'm off for adventure on the high seas and am in need of an extra pair of hands. Would you be willing to come aboard as my first mate this day?'

Jonathan's bleary eyes wandered to the window. 'It's not day. It's the middle of the night. And… (yawn)… I don't even know what a first mate is supposed to do.'

'No excuses, now,' said Father sternly. 'Yea or Nay?'

'I'm not… I don't… ,' stammered Jonathan as he tried to collect his wits and shake the sleep from his head.

I rose and lit the oil lamp. Bretta stretched, yawned, and got up to feed the fire. Elsa didn't stir from her deep sleep. Our cabin awoke in the glow of the combined lights. There stood Father in his sea-faring clothes. In his hand he held two packages tied with string.

'Well now, perhaps this will help you decide,' Father said as he pulled the string on the top package. He unfolded a yellow seaman's slicker that was exactly Jonathan's size. Beneath it was a yellow sou'wester to keep his head and neck dry.

'Wherever did you get this?' I asked, coming over to take a closer look. Jonathan was already out of bed trying on the sou'wester hat. Elsa sat up and stretched. 'Remember I told you about the merchant I met in town the day before yesterday? The one who gave me a present? Well, this is it. He had it special made for his daughter, but she never wore it. His wife refused to let him take her to sea.'

Jonathan took off the hat and looked at it.

'Now Jonathan, don't go turning up your nose because it was made for a girl,' said Father. 'It's true seaman's make with seams tight as a ship's hull.'

'What is in the other package?' I asked.

Father pulled the string and began pulling out articles of clothing: long johns, wool socks with cotton liners, flannel-lined storm pants, turtleneck and wool shirt, and a double-breasted pea coat. Last came a wool cap that would fit under the sou'wester. Jonathan's expression became more surprised with the unveiling of each article. The girls came close and ran their hands over the garments.

'Father, these are new!' cried Bretta.

Elsa became very excited. 'Did you bring new clothes for us, too, Father? Clothes from Anderson's Store? The blue dress! Surely you brought the blue dress I showed you last December!'

Father knelt down in front of Elsa but did not touch her. 'These clothes are lent to me on credit by Mr. Andersen. He feels sure my profit will increase with the boy's help. As do I.'

Elsa stopped. She looked down and tears welled from her eyes and rolled down her face.

Father did take her hand then. 'Elsa, take heart. Perhaps we will have fineries some day. But for right now look for the joy in all that does surround you. Don't let the desire of some material good snatch away your happiness.'

Still holding Elsa's hand, he reached into his pocket with the other. 'You must find delight in the smallest things. Like this spool of thread for example.'

Elsa let out an ecstatic scream and held out her hands into which Father dropped the spool. 'Thread, Mother! Brunda will have her arm again! Oh, when can you show me how to do it? I want to do it myself! Please? Can you show me?'

'After the men have left for the sea, Elsa,' I said.

I nodded to Carl. He had done well. When his eyes met mine I felt pride and love swell from deep within me.

The cart was loaded with fishing nets, buckets, knives, fish lines and hooks, oars, a storm lantern, and a basket of food that would last two hungry men a day. Father put the yoke over his shoulders and adjusted the strap. He looked to the east hoping to see the first signs of dawn, but the sky was still broiling in inky blackness.

Elsa was talking to Jonathan. 'Father has never taken Bretta or me to sea. We used to beg him often, but he would not listen. You are fortunate you are a boy.'

'We will see whether it be fortune or folly,' said Father. He took a few steps to test the balance of the wagon and the adjustment of the yoke.

The girls and I went up and kissed him good-bye. Jonathan stood nearby, watching and twisting his wool cap in his hands. Then he quickly said 'good-by', pulled on his cap and started walking down the path.

'Oh no you don't,' I said as I caught him, picked him up and gave him a big hug. 'Trying to sneak off without a proper good-bye are you?'

I gave him a kiss on his ruddy cheek and set him down in front of Elsa and Bretta.

He took each by the hand and said 'good-bye for now.' They wished him good fishing and good weather, and he was off following Father down the path.

I stayed at home with the girls, of course, so must tell this next part second hand.

⤳

It was still dark after walking for a half an hour. However the early hour and moonless dark did nothing to dampen Jonathan's excitement. He nearly danced around Father.

'Will we be out to sea for weeks and months? Will we harpoon any whales? How big is your ship? Does it have cannons? I would dearly like to shoot off a cannon!'

Father laughed. It was a deep, joyful sound, rarely heard.

The cold morning suddenly turned frigid. The merest glimmer of predawn was sucked into darkness.

A voice came from around a turn in the path. 'You sound rather happy for a man who is about to die.'

Father stopped. His face clouded over. Jonathan could tell by his expression that Father had heard that voice before.

We trudged forward and followed the path around the curve. There, sitting on a rock where the village path crossed a smaller path, was a man dressed in black. The man could only be seen as a dark shadow in the darkness. He lit a white pipe clenched in his teeth and his features were revealed for an instant. His face was criss-crossed with scars and the thick fringe of a beard lined his jaw. There was a rugged handsomeness about him in spite of the scars.

Jonathan caught his breath. He thought for an instant he faced Black Peter again. But no... this man was shorter and had different features.

'Merchantman Rupert,' said Father. 'What are you doing here at the crossroads? Scaring passers by with your storm predictions?'

'You make jest of a serious matter,' the man said with a sincere tone in his voice. 'There is a storm coming. A big one. If you go out, you will drown.'

'Bah!' shouted Father and continued pulling the cart down the path.

As we made another turn in the path, we heard, 'I am only thinking of your safety, and that of your son. What would your wife and daughters do if you were gone?'

When we were further down the path, Jonathan said, 'He seemed pretty sure of himself. Perhaps we should listen to him.'

Father looked as if he would get angry, but then checked himself. Kneeling down on one knee, he looked Jonathan in the eye. 'In truth, boy, there is foul weather afoot. It is likely a small outburst and I judge that it won't hit for three or four days. We are in "danger" of fishing in light rain and choppy waves only. But even if the weather were severe, not a storm mind you, I would still go out.' He held Jonathan's shoulders in his big hands. 'Our store of food is low and we will require money to buy basic foodstuffs. Also, we will need to keep part of the catch for our own pot. I hope and pray with your help we will profit above the cost of staples. We have the season to consider… Christmas feast and all.'

Father patted Jonathan's shoulder and stood up. 'You must know I wouldn't take you out there if there were any danger. This trip will most likely be wet and cold, and I wished for better on your first voyage at sea. But it can't be helped.'

As they continued to walk, Father told Jonathan about the business at hand. 'Yesterday when I went to the village, I rowed out three miles and set four hook lines. Today we must haul up those lines and the fish they have caught. Each line is very long and is set with 500 hooks. Your job is to turn the crank of the winch while I take the fishes off and toss them in the correct buckets. Without your help I would only be able to haul two lines in a day, turning the crank myself and stopping to free the fish from the hooks.'

'That doesn't sound adventurous in the least,' said Jonathan.

Father laughed his deep laugh again. 'We shall see.'

They reached the village as dawn broke over the land. Jonathan looked out to sea. The clouds on the eastern horizon lit up with a cold glow. When the sun pushed its way up, it appeared as a pale, deformed oval. Its diffuse light shed no warmth.

The path widened into a dirt road and led directly to the wharf. We passed a row of warehouses and empty stands where fish would be sold later in the day. Finally we came to perhaps the cheeriest building in the village, the Bait & Hook Inn. Father unhitched the yoke from his shoulders.

'Stay out here and look after the cart,' he said. 'I need to hear the latest news, find who has had success and where, and discuss the weather signs a bit. I won't be long.'

Father had only just entered the front door when Jonathan heard a cold voice from behind him. 'Well, well… 'tis the son of Carl the fisherman.'

'I'm not his…' Jonathan cut short as he spun around. He came face-to-face with the man Father had called 'Merchantman Rupert.'

'Y-you are Black Peter,' Jonathan stammered. 'Your face is scarred and your moustache is gone, your clothes are changed and the dreadful horned head piece is gone, but you are the one who stole me away from my mother!'

'Aye,' he said, 'and here I am known as "Knecht Rupert" the merchant. In other places "Hans Trapp" or "Krampus" or… "Black Peter", to name just a few. I have been called by many names since I fell from grace.'

Black Peter glanced from side to side. In a low voice he said, 'I will come to you later this day with a task for you to perform. Be prepared to act swiftly and do exactly as I ask.'

'What makes you think I will do your bidding?' asked Jonathan.

'I know you will, for I have the power to reward you,' his mouth curved into an evil smile, 'by granting you that which you most desire.'

At that very moment, Father came bursting out of the Bait & Hook. He was followed by an older fisherman who was slapping him on the back and saying, 'Just keep your storm slicker buckled tight and you'll be fine.'

The fisherman was a little taller than Father and thin but for a slightly rounded paunch. His hair and full beard were snowy white and were worn long. He also wore a moustache unlike most fishermen, who shaved their upper lips.

Another fisherman came out the door, puffing on a huge pipe. He was the shortest of the three and was dressed for the sea in a yellow slicker and sou'wester just like Jonathan's. His round face was rimmed with a short beard the color of dark chocolate. The Fisherman said nothing, but merely looked up at the lowering sky.

'Jonathan,' said Father, 'here are two friends, Kristopher Nicks and Steamer McCullough.'

Jonathan shook hands with the taller and shorter fisherman in turn. The eyes of the taller one, Kristopher Nicks, sparkled in the gloomy light as he bent to take Jonathan's hand as if there were some hidden jest in their meeting. Steamer McCullough's grip was painfully strong, but his smile around the stump of his pipe was very cheery.

'So this is your boy,' Mister Nicks said. Then in an aside to Father he said, 'A little scrawny, an't he? Sure he'll pull his weight?'

Father looked down at Jonathan with a slight curve at the corners of his mouth. 'There is more to this little master than meets the eye. He will do quite handily.'

Jonathan smiled at this. His smile faded in a flash as he remembered Black Peter. He spun around, but the bearded man in black was gone.

Father rowed with mighty strokes that sped the dory seaward. Jonathan was amazed how quickly the boat had been readied with the help of Misters Nicks and McCullough. It was launched and in a short while Father's vigor had brought them far enough that the land was but a dark line behind them.

'I had imagined a larger boat,' Jonathan said above the growling wind. The Dory was eighteen feet long, flat bottomed, and filled with large buckets, nets ropes fishing lines, small wooden boxes, and one basket of food.

'I also imagined it would be a *sailing* vessel.'

'This is a sturdy boat and a quick one in calm weather. It does the job,' Father said between his heaving at the oars.

Jonathan was filled with awe at the vastness of the sea. As they continued out, he became fearful. Their small craft drifted above an immeasurable abyss, dark as death. Huge, round-shouldered waves rolled about them, unaffected by their insignificant presence.

Jonathan gripped the rail and cringed in the wake of an oncoming wave. It sent a shower of cold water into the dory. Glancing at Father, Jonathan noticed he was unconcerned. Jonathan tried to be the same.

When they were completely out of sight of land, Father stopped and peered over the side into the depths. Nodding, he shipped the oars and made ready to cast the nets.

'I thought you said something about pulling up lines with a winch,' Jonathan said.

'That comes later,' Father said, grunting as he cast the first net. 'First we must catch smaller fishes to rebait the lines.'

He cast the second net. 'Should be a short wait. Just enough time for a cup of coffee.' He sat and pulled the basket of provisions to him. Opening the lid he pulled out an earthenware jug with a corked top. Uncorking it, he poured two mugs of steaming coffee.

As they sipped at the mugs, Jonathan could see the thick black clouds above them form into towering thunderheads. The wan light of the morning sun illuminated their features briefly with dramatic highlights. Then the wind increased and caused the sun to be obscured.

Father gazed up over the rim of his mug and his eyebrows lowered in angry surprise. He lowered the mug and gazed over the seascape, watching the waves increase in proportion to the strength of the wind.

Father stood and began to haul in the nets. As he did, Jonathan heard him say under his breath, 'If that merchant proves to be the harbinger of bad luck, I'll have him strung up by his tongue.'

The first net had nothing, but the second brought up enough to fill two buckets.

'That will do,' said Father as he sat down and grabbed the oars again. It began to rain. The dory rose and slid in hills and valleys of dark waters. Father yelled for Jonathan to bail out some of the water that flowed over the rail. Jonathan feared to let go of the rail. His eyes were wide with panic and his gaze followed the rise and fall of the sea.

'Straddle the board and grip it with your legs,' Father shouted. 'Good. Now use the closest bucket.'

Jonathan threw buckets of water over the side. He had cleared all but an inch or so of water when the sea seemed to calm.

'See, Jonathan,' Father said, easing his powerful strokes, 'not much more than a mist and a bit of roll, is all. Just as I said.'

Jonathan dropped the bucket and gripped the seat, breathing hard. A sudden rise made his breath stutter in his throat. 'Father, we must go back. Now. I am afraid we will turn over and drown. We are all alone out here. No one to help us.'

Carl was taken aback. It was the first time Jonathan had called him 'Father.' He shipped the oars and climbed forward to sit opposite Jonathan. In doing so, the dory stopped its forward motion and began to flounder.

'Jonathan…'

'Please, Father! The merchant was right, only he isn't a merchant, he is Black Peter and I think he has power over the sea and he will make his own prediction about the storm come true and then we will drown…'

'Hold, Jonathan, hold,' said Father in a deep, calm voice. He steadied Jonathan, gripping him with his big hands. 'You're letting fear take you over. The merchant is only a man, a foolish man. He has only the power of fear and vexation. Set these frights aside and let us look to our work, for soon comes the hardest test.'

He let his arms drop, but kept his eyes on Jonathan's. 'Are you ready? Are you able?'

Jonathan looked down and said in a voice so small the wind almost swept it away. 'The sea is so vast and we are so small. It could crush us with a single wave whether the wave be called by Peter or no.'

'This is true,' Father said. He moved back to the oars. 'So we will either win or lose. Which do you choose to strive for then, my lad?'

Jonathan looked up and saw Father smiling grimly. He was framed by the lowering sky and was tossed about by the mounting sea. The answer was easy.

'Row on, Father.'

Another hour of rowing brought them in sight of Father's line marker: a net full of stoppered tins with a tall yellow flag jutting from the top. The weather had been getting steadily worse. Rain came down heavily now and Jonathan bailed without pause.

Father rowed to the marker and shipped the oars. Crouching low in the pitching boat, he opened one of the wooden boxes and took out the winch. He clipped it into a metal bracket on the rail and reached for the line marker. As he threaded the fishing line in the winch post, he called over his shoulder, 'Stay low, Jonathan. Do not stand. I don't want to be fishing you out of the sea.

'We will bring in two lines. Three if the weather allows,' he shouted. 'We will probably lose the fourth altogether, but it can't be helped. I will need you to turn the crank steadily for a great length of time. Can you do it?'

'I will try,' called Jonathan. He came forward and grasped the winch handle.

'Now!' shouted Father. 'And do not stop!'

The clack of the winch could barely be heard above the fury about them. The wind howled and tore at Jonathan's yellow storm slicker. Waves thudded and crashed with fearful might over the sides of the boat. Father kept one eye on the line as he bailed a few more buckets of water.

The hooks began to come up and father set the bucket down. He crouched, focusing his attention over the starboard side. Flashes of silver from the depths signaled the approach of the catch. The first three hooks brought up a beautiful ocean perch each, but then hook after hook came with the bait nibbled or gone, or in one case with the remains of a fish a larger fish had attacked. Occasionally a bottle or brick would come up. Father had tied these on the lines to keep them from drifting in the depths.

Fish began coming up again. First two small haddock. The next hook brought up a huge mackerel.

'Look at this! Look at this mackerel!' Father shouted over his shoulder. He used his gaffe to steady the big fish as he pried the hook loose from its mouth. 'This will bring such a price at market!'

All about them the wind and waves raged. Rain poured in sheets from the broiling thunderheads above, but the two of them were so bent on their work they took no notice of it. Jonathan cranked the winch ever faster in anticipation of what might appear next even though his arms ached terribly.

Jonathan looked at Father with new-found admiration. The big man freed fish after fish with practiced efficiency. His large hands were cracked and calloused from years of handling fish, hooks, lines, knives, and gaffs. The irregularities stood out in high relief as the skin on his hands turned white with exposure to the cold and seawater. Father did not seem to notice. He chanted a sea chantey tunelessly as he worked. He turned with a full smile and a wink for Jonathan in between hooks.

Father stood up suddenly and leaned over the side. 'Jonathan, oh Jonathan!' he yelled with glee. 'Wait till you see this next one! A treasure if there ever was one! It will make the entire trip worthwhile. You may have to pause while I cut it free.'

Jonathan was never to know what the treasure was, for at that moment a massive wave crashed over the boat. For what seemed like an eternity, Jonathan tumbled in the water not knowing whether he was in the boat or in the sea, or even which direction was up.

His head bumped into something hard and he grabbed for it. It was a thwart close to the bow of the boat. He had not been swept over!

Kneeling down hip-deep in water, he screamed, 'Father! Father, where are you?'

'I'll tell you where he is,' the calm, sweet voice came from behind him.

It was Black Peter! He was sitting on a sharp finger of rock jutting above the breakers.

A rock that had not been there before. The waves churned wildly about the rock, but not a drop touched his fine boots.

'Black Peter!… But how…?'

'No time for stupid questions, boy. The fisherman is below the water over there,' he indicated the far side of the dory.

Just then Father's head burst through the surface of the water. 'Jonathan!' He coughed and gasped for air. 'I have the line! Turn…'

But he was buried by another wave.

'I have come with my task,' Black Peter continued as if nothing of importance was going on.

'But he will die!'

'Which brings us to the point,' he said insistently. 'Perform this thing for me and I will take you back to your true mother instantly.'

Jonathan's mouth gaped.

'Yes, from this very spot I will take you to the warmth of your mother's embrace. To your room full of toys. To your beautiful house full of beautiful things.'

There was a 'woosh' of breath behind Jonathan and Father's weakened voice saying, '… crank! … turn…'

Jonathan's voice came from his throat flat as death, 'What do you want?'

Black Peter smiled.

'Cut the line and let the man drown.'

↜

A battle ensued. Not a battle of swords or guns. Or even fists.

It was a battle of a boy alone in the sea fighting off an onslaught of foul persuasion. His assailant, the master of lies, attacked him with weapons honed by ages of malevolent application.

The onslaught battered the boy's senses from within and without. The devil tore at the child's deepest feelings without mercy. All the while, the child struggled.

Struggled even as his heart and mind were horribly battered.

Struggled to save the life of one he loved.

CHAPTER 6
In the Village

Father lay on the white bed, cold and still. I sat in a chair by his side. My left hand gently clasping his clammy right hand. I wished with all my might that his eyes would open, though I knew it was in vain.

Kristopher Nicks had set out to fetch me as soon as the foul weather had turned angry. Before he left, he asked Steamer McCullough to take his tug out and make sure Carl and Jonathan got home safe. McCullough's thirty-five foot tug had a steam engine and was heavy enough to weather a small storm.

Mister Nicks' long stride made quick work of the long walk to our cabin. The way back took longer with the girls in tow. I was amazed how spry was Mister Nicks at his advanced years. He even carried Elsa for a while when she became too tired to run.

I was on the docks when Mister McCullough returned with Jonathan and Father's boat in tow. Father was in the cabin of the tug, wrapped in a blanket like an Egyptian mummy. Jonathan cradled Father's head in his lap. His face was stoic, almost severe.

'It's all my fault,' Mister McCullough kept saying. 'I'm the one who first told him the weather would be tolerable.'

'Nonsense,' Kristopher Nicks said as he helped carry Father from the docks down Wide Street to the Captain's Table Inn. 'I added my assurance as well.' He had looked up at the sky then as in angry disbelief.

Others who had been on the docks and followed us to the Captain's Table tried to comfort Mister McCullough as well. Jonathan held his hand and thanked him again and again for coming out to rescue them. Still he would not be cheered.

Doctor Fezzic had been sent for as soon as we saw Father in Mister McCullough's arms. He arrived just as we laid Father in Miss Marie's best down-stairs room. The doctor shooed everyone out of the room and insisted that we sit quietly in the Common Room. Miss Marie served hot coffee to all as we waited.

Jonathan was fatigued but insisted on telling me what had happened. 'We were well underway in our efforts when Father was washed overboard by a big wave. He was able to grab the fishing line as he went, but the high seas made it impossible to regain the boat. I cranked the winch hoping to bring him in by the line.' Jonathan paled and he swallowed with difficulty. 'The twine slid in his grip and the closest hook snagged his hand, piercing completely through it.'

I laid a hand over Jonathan's mouth as my head swam for a moment. I shut my eyes and then nodded for him to continue.

'I was able to bring him close,' Jonathan said, 'but before I could help him into the swamped boat, another large wave came from the opposite direction and slammed his head against the bow.' Jonathan gritted his teeth and looked grim.

It was then that Kristopher Nicks reached out to put an arm around his shoulders. 'You did not give up then did you, though you *both* were under siege.'

Jonathan looked up quickly at that. He looked into the old fisherman's eyes and saw a sparkle of understanding there.

'No,' Jonathan said. 'I couldn't! But neither could I lift Father into the boat. He was far too heavy for me. It was all I could do to keep his head above water.

'A third huge wave tore Father from my grip. Neither could the hook in his hand keep him in such chaos. I could see his yellow slicker under the water as he drifted away from the boat. In the commotion I hadn't heard Mister McCullough's tug boat come upon us.' Jonathan looked to where Steamer McCullough sat. 'He had his boat about, his gaff in the water, and Father on deck before I could cry out.'

At that a great cheer erupted from the villagers and many patted Steamer's back and toasted him with cups of coffee.

Dr. Fezzic came out, angrily hushing the crowd. The wild white hair on his head quivered as he lowered his gaze. I ran to him and actually had the nerve to cup his chin in my hand and lift his eyes to mine.

'Tell me, sir,' I said.

'Sorry, m'dear' he said through a white moustache that covered his mouth. 'I am over tired. Your husband is suffering from exposure to cold, a nasty gash in his right hand, and a concussion. He also swallowed a good deal of seawater and inhaled some as well, though the latter has been entirely cleared.' He stopped and looked around at the expectant faces. 'Well, there it is. You can all go home now.'

There was a momentary silence. Then a dozen voices spoke at once, mine perhaps the loudest. 'Will he survive?'

Doctor Fezzic held up his hand. 'Silence. Silence, please! For the good of all.' He caught his breath. 'Yes. YES. With proper rest he will be on his feet in a week.'

Such a cheer arose from the crowd that Steamer McCullough could not suppress a close-lipped smile. They picked him up and Jonathan too. They carried them both out the front door, turning toward the center of the village shouting and cheering. Oh, the villagers will tell and retell this story for years to come.

Jonathan never did tell them the full tale concerning Black Peter and all. He did tell me at the urging of Kristopher Nicks. Jonathan returned to the inn where I sat alone with Carl and told me everything starting with the meeting of Merchantman Ruppert at the crossroads. I must admit I was skeptical that Krampus would disguise himself as a merchant and pursue one small child.

It was discovered later that Knecht Ruppert had disappeared from the village leaving a hired room at the Bait & Hook completely torn apart.

～

Father remained at the Captain's Table at the insistence of the owner, Miss Marie.

Jonathan and I collected the girls from Mister and Missus Andersen's, who had offered to keep them while I saw to Father. The girls begged to be allowed to see Father before we had to leave. I relented with their promise to peek quietly from the doorway.

Mister Andersen accompanied us back to the inn. The girls were good to their word although Elsa sobbed noiselessly at the sight of Father lying so forlorn and alone. I had to pull them away and silently shut the door.

'What will you do now that your Mister is unable to work and his latest catch is lost?' asked Mister Anderson kindly.

I shook my head. I had no answer.

'Mother,' cried Bretta, 'the Christmas ornaments we made… couldn't we give them to Mr. Andersen to sell in his store?'

'Oh Bretta, I don't think…' I began.

'This is a wonderful idea!' Mister Andersen said. 'I often receive requests for seasonal ornaments. I could also use a few Christmas trees if you could manage it.'

'I believe we could fit three small trees in Father's cart,' Jonathan said. 'I am an expert at selecting the most excellent trees. I'm sure I can find three in the forest.'

'And there is more that we could produce given two or three days,' Elsa said excitedly.

'Ah, my dears, I would wish for your goods in two days,' said Mister Andersen. 'Christmas is just around the corner after all!'

'Done!' said Jonathan and shook Mister Andersen's hand heartily, much to the amusement of all.

We bid Mister Andersen good-bye with many thanks. Kristopher Nicks showed up at the inn door with Father's cart in tow. The yoke was snuggly settled on his shoulders.

'The daylight wanes,' he said, eyes twinkling in the dusk. 'May I offer the children a ride home?'

'Thank you, sir, but I couldn't bear to have you walk that long path again,' I said.

Mister Nicks held out for a bit, but finally surrendered the cart to me. The girls climbed in and Jonathan stood by my side. We waved goodbye to Mister Nicks and Miss Marie, who leaned out the kitchen window. We were off.

The children talked excitedly about our business venture for a wile and then grew silent as first Elsa and then Bretta fell asleep in the cart. Jonathan stumbled on for another half hour before I insisted that he join the girls in the cart. It was a bit hard to pull that amount of weight, but I didn't mind. Precious cargo is never a burden.

The two days passed quickly. We worked at such a pace we had little time to think of else. Mister McCullough came by each afternoon to give us the best fish of his catch for our supper and to tell us of Father's progress. We would send our love back with him.

Our industry began on the first morning by loading the cart with ornaments we had already made for our own house: two evergreen wreaths and a long garland, a pinecone centerpiece, and a carving of Santa Claus father had done two years ago. Jonathan found three pine saplings within sight of our porch. He had them cut and tied to the sides of the cart with net twine in half a day. Elsa and Bretta gathered aromatic leaves, pine needles, nuts and flowers from the forest and made sachets. I created more wreaths, adorning each with red bows I made from scraps died in ground hollyberry.

The second day began with the discovery of a real treasure: mistletoe! Jonathan climbed to where it was growing in the high boughs of a cedar. The girls gathered hollyberries and their prickly leaves and we began tying small arrangements of the three. While we sat about the table with our heads bent to our work, Elsa snuck up behind Jonathan and held a sprig of mistletoe over his head. Elsa's giggle caught Bretta's attention and she quickly pecked Jonathan's cheek before he knew what was going on.

'Blah!' he said and shrugged one shoulder to wipe his cheek. This made the girls laugh uproariously.

A morning's hard work filled a bushel basket with mistletoe ornaments. We rested with a midday meal of dried fish and hot water. Jonathan and the girls discussed what else we might make around bites of salted fish.

'Jonathan, can you whittle figures in wood?' asked Bretta. 'Father left a knife and wood on the porch. Perhaps you could make Mary, Joseph and a manger.'

Jonathan looked apprehensive but said he would try.

I went to our pantry box and rummaged through. Finding what I sought, I said, 'What can we do with these?' I brought out nine candles. Elsa squealed and clapped her hands. Bretta was less excited.

'Mother,' she said, 'we need those ourselves. What will we do for light?'

'We will make do with firelight until we can make more,' I answered. 'Now come.

We have left over holly leaves and berries, cedar twigs, and pine ends to adorn the bases.'

Jonathan went out to try his hand at carving wood. He was gone perhaps twenty-five minutes before he stormed in and threw a misshapen piece of wood on the table.

'I tried Mary first. Ugh!' he said. 'I nearly cut my thumb off and the face looks more like moose than Madonna.'

We all laughed. He looked even angrier and would have screamed for silence, but then Elsa fell off her chair holding her sides and laughing uncontrollably. Jonathan tried to stifle a smile, but ended up laughing with the rest of us.

'Jonathan,' I said, 'go out to the woodpile and select three attractive logs. We'll attach acorns and red bows and call them Yule Logs. This will have to be our last project, or we will not be able to make it to town before Mister Andersen closes his door for the evening.'

It was late in the afternoon before the last of our industry was loaded into Father's cart. Off we went! Jonathan and I pulled while Elsa and Bretta walked behind, helping at need. We sang Christmas carols as we walked, first north through the woods and then east to the crossroads.

When we turned the curve and came in sight of the crossroads where the large granite boulder stood, Jonathan fell silent. We sang on a while before we noticed his solemn mood.

'Are you thinking of your meeting here with Black Peter?' I asked.

'Well, that too,' he said. He thought of something and his head turned to the east where the village was just coming into view.

'Is Santa Claus going to be in the town square?' Jonathan asked in a rush.

The girls giggled. 'Of course not. We won't see him until Christmas Eve,' Bretta said.

'Why do you ask?' Elsa said, dancing around in front of him.

'My mother took me to our village to see Santa last year. I got mad and smacked him in the nose. I wrote him a letter to say I was sorry, but I know he didn't forgive me entirely.' He paused. 'He didn't bring me all the toys I asked for, and then this year... this year he sent Black Peter to take me from my home.'

The girls looked questioningly at me.

'But Mister Claus wouldn't...' Elsa began.

'Black Peter *said*,' snapped Jonathan. 'He said he was captured by St. Nicholas long ago and was bound to do his bidding one night a year.'

Bretta and Elsa stopped and looked at him in disbelief. 'But what did Santa say to you when he came to your house on Christmas Eve?' asked Bretta.

'I've never been able to stay up 'till midnight so that I could see him. Besides, Grammy told me he doesn't like children to see him deliver presents.'

'But that isn't so,' the girls said more or less together. Elsa continued, 'He is always so happy to talk with us on the Eve of Christmas. How was he able to give you his most special gift if he didn't talk to you directly?'

'I'm sure I don't know what you're talking about… special gifts and all, but Grammy wouldn't tell me something that wasn't true.'

'We all know Mister Claus honors different traditions in different parts of the world,' I said. 'It is entirely possible you are both right.'

Jonathan and the girls thought about that for a moment and then, looking at each other's puzzled expressions, burst out laughing.

We continued on into the village.

⌒

'Carl is not here,' Miss Marie said in her scratchy voice.

I felt a sudden lurch in the pit of my stomach. 'Not here? Did the doctor move him to his surgery? Has he taken a turn for the worse?'

'No, no, not at all,' she said. 'Just the opposite in fact. We couldn't keep him at rest. He insisted on going to Andersen's to play checkers.'

My fear turned to irritation. 'Well, I never! Disobeying doctor's orders after but three days recovery.' I bobbed a quick curtsy in respect to Miss Marie and turned with a snap.

'Come children,' I said. 'I need to find a certain addle-witted fisherman and give him a piece of my mind.' Jonathan and the girls looked at one other but dared not giggle. They turned and hurried after me.

Across Wide Street I stumped, turning at the livery and passing the grocers we arrived at Andersen's Dry Goods. I set the cart' yoke down and rushed in, children following me like ducklings. Lars Andersen stood behind the counter, tall, round, balding with large mutton-chop sideburns. He was wearing the apron that always looked like a child's garment on him.

'Merry Christmas, Frieda, and to the handsome children as well,' He said in his jolly voice. 'I have so looked forward to your visit.'

He looked out his large front window. 'I see you have been wondrous busy. Your cart is full and overfull! Let us take a look.'

'A moment,' I said. I took a deep breath and let it out slowly to calm myself. 'I was told my husband is here trying to rehabilitate his injuries by playing checkers.' I looked at the empty chairs by the checkers board. 'Carl, are you here?'

'Carl... Carl...' Mister Andersen said, crossing his arms over his round stomach and touching his index finger to his lips. 'I believe I've heard this name... Oh, yes! The man who is both fisherman and fish, both catcher and catch!' The merry twinkle in his eye fled when he saw my severe expression. 'Perhaps if we check the shelf where I stock my tins of tuna and salmon...'

As I turned around, Father popped from behind the shelving, head and hand thickly bandaged in white. He was making a 'fish mouth' and was pretending to swim.

'Hurrah!' Jonathan and the girls screamed, rushing around me. They skidded to a halt and hugged him all around. I found it hard to remain angry in the light of such a joyful reunion.

'Easy, children,' Father said. 'I still lose my balance easily and my hand gives me terrible pain now and again.' He looked up and saw my stormy expression. 'But, uh... I'm feeling much better. Almost myself you might say.'

'Good,' I said stepping forward, 'because you are about to receive your second concussion.'

'Ha, ha, Ooch,' he squinted and held his good hand to his head. When he opened his eyes, I was right in front of him. 'Frieda, I have missed you so these three days.'

The last shred of my anger drained away. We embraced, yes, right in front of Mister Andersen and the children.

'Harump,' Mister Anderson cleared his throat. 'I am so sorry to spoil your happy reunion with bad news, but I must, my dears.'

We turned around searching his eyes for the jest that was usually hidden there. He looked deadpan serious.

'I... I'm afraid I will be unable to honor our agreement to buy your handicrafts.'

'What… ?' I said.

'It is no use arguing, dears,' Mister Andersen said holding up his hands and looking away. 'My mind has been made up for me on this matter! I am unable to sell your goods in my shop.'

'But you asked to look at our wares in the cart,' I said, my heart sinking.

'Curiosity, is all,' he said and covered his mouth with his big hand.

My mouth worked up and down as I tried to stammer an it's-OK-we-will-manage-somehow, but I just couldn't. We had poured our hearts and souls into our work. Our spirits had been lifted by the promise of hope in the face of disaster. And now…

'Surprise!!' cried a dozen voices as women jumped from behind bolts of cloth and sacks of flour. One of the women stepped forward. It was Kristopher Nicks' wife Merry. Her stout figure was bedecked in the cheeriest red dress with green and white bows and lace trim.

'Mister Anderson is unable to offer your goods in his store because we convinced him to let us buy them direct. Cutting out the middleman, as it were,' she said, poking Lars Andersen in his ample stomach. There was much twittering from behind her at that.

'With your permission, Missus, we'd like to have all the profit go to you and your dear family.'

'Why, yes… of course,' I said. 'If that is quite agreeable to Mister Anderson.'

Sarah McCullough, Steamer's wife, was pulling our cart in through the front door. 'As he said, his mind has been made up for him. Ladies, shall we begin?'

Missus Nicks presided. She would hold up an item so that all could see and say 'What is a fair price for this beauty?' If two in the gathering came up with different prices, the item always sold for the higher of the two. It was not an auction as such. Once a price was set, Mary asked for buyers and she would choose one. This way everyone left that day with a hand-made treasure.

At first I was terribly embarrassed and self-conscious. I felt that the women had gotten together to give us charity out of pity. Carl stood with his good arm around me. He seemed ill at ease as well.

Our minds were put at rest when, as each piece sold, the buyer would come up and compliment us on the fine craft that went into the making. We heard comments like 'my neighbor paid twice as much for something not nearly as nice' and 'I tried to make my own this year, but I just don't have talent like Frieda and her children.'

As the last pine centerpiece was being sold, Kristopher Nicks and Miss Marie came through the front door. They were deep in argument about the Christmas trees that Sarah McCullough had untied and left out front.

'I'll agree to let you take the taller one if you agree to pay one dollar more for it!' Miss Marie was saying.

'Done,' Mister Nicks said and shook her hand as if she were a man.

'I must claim the third tree for myself,' Mister Andersen said and looked about in mock challenge.

Just then Steamer McCullough came in the door carrying a half carved branch. 'Is this moose taken?'

Jonathan eyes flew wide. 'What… who… how?' he sputtered. He looked angrily at the girls. Elsa had her mouth covered with one hand. She was pointing at her sister with the other. Bretta was smiling like a cat with a mouthful of canary.

'And now, friends,' Mister Andersen's voice boomed over the gathering, 'business is finished for the day. Let the merriment begin!' He drew back the curtain behind the counter and out stepped his wife, Peg, and his two sons, Erik and Sean. They were carrying trays of goblets and a steaming bowl of wassail. Following them came three men carrying instruments: fiddle, tin whistle, and drum. The musicians began 'Here We Come A Wassailing' as the Andersens served.

When the song finished, Mister Andersen raised his cup. 'To all of us on this happy day and in this wonderful season! May friendship ever prevail. Wassail!'

'Wassail,' we shouted together and drained our cups.

The musicians started up a merry jig that set some to dancing, some to singing, and all to tapping their toes. We danced and sang the late afternoon into evening. I believe I talked with everyone there and everyone who came in the door thereafter.

Father didn't dance, of course, but he did clap his good hand upon his thigh, sing, and he did join in the merry conversations with lively vigor. The children did dance. They danced with such happy abandon that it brought many an amused chuckle from those in the gathering.

At odd times, Carl and I would discuss what we should buy with the profit of the day. Father was in charge of resupplying our pantry with needed foodstuffs. I took charge of the remainder. It was my job to purchase dry goods and to dole out the rest to the children. It was up to them to decide what materials they needed to make Christmas presents.

I gathered them and gave them each a budget. Elsa needed Bretta to add numbers for her, but Jonathan having had some schooling went off on his own. He came back moments later with a beautiful tree top angel in his hands.

'This can be my present to you and Father,' he said.

'It's a handsome ornament and no doubt, Jonathan, but there are two things you might consider' I said looking at the price tag. 'First this costs more than your limit,' I said. 'Second...'

'You can take some from the dry goods money, can't you? I really want this for the family.'

'Second, take a look at these.' I persisted, picking up a few items from a nearby counter: a stick of paraffin, a small roll of wide lace, a box of starch, and primary color craft paints and brush. 'What do you see?'

'A few odds and ends, why?' he said.

'I see an angel much prettier than yours at one tenth the price,' I said. 'I see a gift of the heart and hand. Something not easily gotten and therefore more treasured by them as get it.'

Jonathan looked from the items in my hands and back at the angel in his. He nodded as if he made a decision. Turning, he put the angel back on the ornaments shelf and disappeared at the back of the store. It was not long before he appeared once more. In his hands was a large bar of soap.

I raised my eyebrows in silent question.

'This is all I want,' he said. 'It's two pennies.'

'Done,' I said, setting the soap carefully in the basket with my own items. I wanted to tell him how we made our own lye soap, but he seemed so determined and the cost was slight.

At last it was time to leave for home. Most of the revelers had left and those that hadn't were wrapping up in scarves and coats in preparation for the cold outside. We settled our bill with Mister Andersen, and loaded our empty cart with a surprisingly large amount of purchases. Miss Marie invited us to stay at the Captain's Table for the night. We thanked her for her offer of hospitality, but said we longed for home. Father said he felt fit enough to make the long walk and thanked Miss Marie again for looking after him and for the use of her beautiful room.

As we set off into the night, Lars Anderson and his family shouted 'Merry Christmas' and waved. Villagers leaned out their windows as we passed saying 'Good Health' and 'God Speed.' We had left the village proper and were well on our way to the edge of the forest when we heard Kristopher Nicks' rich voice shout 'Merry Christmas to you. I will see you soon!'

We were almost home when it began to snow. A hush fell over the wood as winter clothed it in a beautiful trousseau of white. We hiked through the last of the forest and came in sight of our tiny cabin in the clearing.

Jonathan smiled and said, 'Home at last.'

CHAPTER 7
The Spirit of Christmas Arrives

Breakfast the next morning was glorious! Bretta baked Victorian Cake with Elsa's help. I made whipped eggs and Father carved slices of salted pork. Jonathan followed Father's every move and questioned him about the use of a knife.

At last we all sat at table, heads bowed in thanks. Then everyone started talking at once. 'Can we eat like this every morning from now on?', 'Is there money left over for more provisions later?', 'When will you be well enough to go to sea again Father?', 'Isn't this cake the most delicious thing in the world?', and on it went for a full five minutes. Finally father knocked the butt of his knife on the table as if it were a gavel.

'Let us now put our heads together,' he said, 'and decide on what should be done before Christmas Eve.'

'First we must make ornaments for our own house,' I said, 'to replace the ones we sold. I hope we are not too tired of the craft.'

'Oh, of course not', 'Not at all', and 'We are experts now', came from the children.

Jonathan stood up and said, 'I could cut a Christmas tree just for us. I saw one by the path that would be perfect.'

'No need, Jonathan,' Father said. 'Santa always brings a tree with him on Christmas Eve. But if you like, I will show you how to carve with a knife. Perhaps we could make a Santa.'

Jonathan's quizzical face turned to surprise and joy. 'I'd love that! I've had some experience already, so it should be easy.'

'Yes,' said Bretta, 'If you're carving a Christmas Moose, he's your man.'

Jonathan squawked and chased Bretta about the room. It was done in such good humor, I laughed. Father caught them both in his strong arms and said, 'If you quarrel I will have to make you kiss and make up.' Bretta made a face like she had just tasted lemon and Jonathan spit on his hand and wiped his mouth. This made us all laugh.

When the laughter died down, I said, 'We will need ornaments for Santa's tree as well. Bretta can make bread dough figurines and Elsa and I will string popcorn. If Father and Jonathan are able to make wooden ornaments that are light in weight, we will hang them as well.'

I stood and collected breakfast dishes. 'After these tasks are done *then* we may work on projects to give one another as gifts. Not before, mind you.'

We were all so excited to begin that breakfast dishes, pots, pans, and silverware were cleaned in record time. We then bundled up and went into the forest to cut boughs for wreaths, garlands, swags, and a table centerpiece. The girls gathered more holly leaves and berries and Jonathan climbed to get a perfect sprig of mistletoe.

Back at home, Father and Jonathan worked on the wreath, tying the boughs together, attaching small pinecones, red ribbon and a small silver bell given to us by the village smith. The girls and I made the centerpiece, placing a candle in the center, tying it with white and red ribbon. A long garland was worked on by all and draped over the mantle. Finally, I shooed Father and Jonathan out onto the porch to begin their whittling lessons while the girls and I used the last of the pine boughs to decorate the walls.

Making ornaments for the tree came next. Bretta mixed, kneaded, cut and baked bread dough animals. Elsa and I popped and strung popcorn and then worked on a surprise for Jonathan.

After a while, Father and Jonathan came in with small chips of carved wood they claimed were snowflakes. We set all the ornaments on a shelf to await Christmas Eve. All the ornaments but one, that is. The ornament that was to be Jonathan's surprise was hidden under a cloth on the table.

I called him over and Elsa held his eyes while I uncovered it. Father and Bretta 'Ooh-ed' and 'Aah-ed' while Elsa teased Jonathan by refusing to uncover his eyes. Finally he snatched Elsa's hands away.

There on the table stood a beautiful little angel. The face, hands, and wings were fashioned from paraffin and painted with craft paints. They were attached to gown and sleeves made of starched eyelet lace. Finally, some of my own hair had been painstakingly rooted a few strands at a time into the paraffin head.

Jonathan looked up at me and leaned to the side to see where I had cut my own hair. 'I see now.' He looked back at the angel. 'I think real angels must look just like this. All except for the hair. This angel's hair is prettier by far.'

Then came a time of secret projects. Father spent much of the time out in the wood. Jonathan disappeared behind the house for an hour here and there, coming in when his hands got too cold to work. I had a difficult time hiding what I was knitting, but the girls were often busy working and giggling underneath one of the sleeping palates, so I made good progress in a short while.

Christmas Eve arrived!

The girls talked excitedly now and again about Christmases past. At dinner they could talk of nothing else.

Jonathan finally said, 'You have told me all about Santa Claus's visits: his greetings, the spirits he brought with him, the funny things his elves did, and the tales he told you. You have talked about everything except what he *brought* you! What gifts did he give you? You have but one doll between you. No clothes save the ones your mother has stitched together from old rags. You have no books, candies, toys, bicycles, hats, jewelry, or even money!'

His voice was becoming more and more exasperated. 'I don't think Santa stops here at all. If he did you would have all these things and more. You would truly have bounty in your lives,' he looked around, 'instead of poverty and want.'

I looked up from cleaning the stew pot. 'You have forgotten, or perhaps never knew, that there was one who had none of these things you consider so dear, and yet was rich beyond measure. At birth he had not a cradle but a wooden manger filled with straw. During his short life in this world he never became wealthy, nor did he seek to become so. Yet his name will never fade from the memory of man. It is his day of birth we honor this night and this season.'

Father set down a chair he had moved to the fire. 'And Santa Claus, who is a true descendent of the spirit of St. Nicholas, travels the world distributing presents to magnify the joy that abounds in this season.'

I looked from Father to Jonathan. 'Just wait till you see him this night!' I said. 'His whole being shines! He brims with magnificence as you've never seen before.'

'It's so, Jonathan!' Elsa said. 'You'll see.'

Father spoke again. 'You say you've never stayed up to see him, Jonathan? You will not miss him tonight. I promise you.'

The look on Jonathan's face gave me to know he was more worried that Santa *would* come than wouldn't.

⌒

So many stories to tell. So many carols to sing. Dancing and clapping, and of course the most hilarious performance of the evening: Father's rendition of 'Missus Murphy's Christmas Cake.' He sang and accompanied himself with spoons clapping together on his knee, and I would hold up a comb folded over with oilpaper to his mouth for the bits in between the verses. I could barely hold the makeshift kazoo steady I was laughing so hard.

Father had begun a version of 'God Rest Ye Merry, Gentlemen' when he was interrupted by a commotion outside on the roof. Jonathan jumped up in surprise and alarm.

'The roof,' he shouted, 'it's going to cave in.'

'Calm yourself, Jonathan,' I said. 'The roof is stout and strong; it has endured the stress of these visits year after year. It will survive at least one more, I think.'

Then we heard the bells and the pawing of hooves on the turf roof. The bell sounds were like and yet unlike sleigh bells. The bright ringing rippled in harmonies and rhythms like nothing Jonathan had ever heard; it was far removed from the random jangling of mortal bells.

Bretta and Elsa danced about letting out squeals of excitement. Father and I stood up, holding hands. Jonathan looked about nervously.

'The fire,' he said. 'Shouldn't we douse it?'

'No,' said Father. 'Just watch… the fire presents no hazard for Mister Claus.'

There came a soft scraping noise from the chimney shaft. Scuffing and rasping crescendoed into a long scrape. Suddenly there was a burst of brilliant sparks as if the Yule log had exploded and there stood Santa Claus, arms outstretched.

He had a small smudge of soot on his nose and a cloud of ash drifted from his shoulders like a gray evening cape. On the floor by his feet sat a large sack made of the same red suede as his suit. The trim on his hat and coat was jet black and bristled like bear's fur.

'Oh my dear family,' he said in a rich, jovial voice, 'how I have looked forward to seeing you again! And Jonathan…' his voice trailed off, but this went unnoticed in the rush to embrace him. Elsa, Bretta, and I reached him first, then Father, towering over Santa, hugged the four of us at once. Jonathan stood alone.

'Come Jonathan,' Santa said over Elsa's head. 'You have earned a place here and earned it well. We are heartily proud of you. Yes indeed!'

Jonathan stepped closer, but did not join in.

Suddenly everyone was talking. I was saying what a help the girls had been this year and how responsible they had grown. Elsa and Bretta were telling Santa all the exciting events of the year. Father was saying something about his Special Gift and something else about nets.

'Ho Ho HO-O-o-o!' Santa laughed with genuine amusement. 'I wish to hear it all, but *not* at once, if you don't mind. Ho-ho, ho-ho!'

Everyone stopped and then laughed. We were embarrassed that our excitement had overcome our manners. Santa was holding his round stomach and laughing heartily. When he finally stopped, he said, 'Elsa, dear little one, would you please fetch the pitcher and a mug?'

'Yes Santa,' Elsa said with a curtsey. She ran to the shelf and returned with the empty pitcher and one of the heavy mugs.

'How I would love a cup of the fine tea made from the children's dried herbs,' said Santa. 'I smelt it on St. Lucia's day and have desired a taste ever since.'

Jonathan spoke up saying, 'But it's all gone and we haven't collected or dried herbs…'

But Santa was already tipping the pitcher towards his cup. Steaming tea poured into the mug and its spicy aroma filled the room. 'Ahhhh!' he said waving the cup under his nose. 'But I couldn't drink without company! Join me! The children's tea promises to be better than the best.'

Jonathan didn't move. He just stood there staring at the pitcher with his mouth open. Elsa and Bretta ran to get more mugs. They gave one to me and one to Father, and as Bretta handed one to Jonathan I heard her whisper, 'Close your mouth and be polite.'

Santa filled each mug, set the pitcher down and raised his own cup in toast. "Merry Christmas! May God bless us every one!' He sipped from his cup eyeing Jonathan from behind the rim.

'Merry Christmas,' we echoed and drained our cups. Jonathan peered into his mug, sniffed, and then with a shrug, drank.

'Now,' said Santa, lighting a pipe he had pulled from thin air with a match that had come from the same place, 'tell me *everything.*'

We each had our turn, starting with father. He thanked Santa for the gift of net designs and the marine twine with which to make them. He told of his successes at sea and how the increased prosperity helped us live more comfortably. I saw Jonathan glance about when Father said this. Perhaps he was imagining how we lived with less income.

I then told Santa all the things Bretta and Elsa had learned in the ways of cooking, baking, sewing and knitting. I thanked him for the instruction on how to knit the warmest socks and for giving me the yarn to make pairs for the family.

Bretta and Elsa alternated telling Santa endlessly about small things that they had been interested in this year. Everything from what new games they devised to who they talked to in the village and what they said.

'Elsa and Bretta, don't forget your "thank-yous",' I reminded.

'Oh yes!' Elsa said excitedly. 'Thank you for your special gift that came to pass on May Day. I rose early as you instructed and went to the clearing in the forest where the creek runs close to the white pine. It was as beautiful a morning as could be and I thought to myself, 'This is what Santa wanted to give me: a morning so pretty I'll always remember it.'

'Then I saw a fawn walk through the clearing. It looked to be heading for the creek to get a drink. I must have made a small noise, for it stopped and turned its face to me, ears all perked up. I didn't move, but it was looking right at me. Then, miracle of miracles, it walked right up to where I was standing and sniffed and nuzzled me all over! Even when I laughed, it didn't run away!'

'It was a special gift indeed,' Elsa finished in a quiet voice.

'Mine too, Santa,' said Bretta, 'even though it didn't seem like much of a special gift when you presented the plan to me.

'I baked the honey cakes with the recipe you gave early on the morning of March 30th and put them in a basket. I walked to the village and arrived at Miss Marie's inn, The Captain's Table, in the early afternoon. Elsa came with me. When Miss Marie came to the door, I did exactly as you said; I uncovered the honey cakes and said 'This is in remembrance.

'At first I thought I had done it all wrong, for she broke out in tears. When she collected herself and apologized, she explained how March 30th was the day ten years past that she lost her husband and only son at sea. She said none of the village folk ever talked much about her loss for fear of causing her sorrow to come back anew. The truth was that she wanted to talk about them, show photographs and mementos of their lives and remember how they had been the heart and soul of her life.

'And so she did, well into the late afternoon. She prepared an early dinner so we would be able to make it home before dark. She served my honey cakes for dessert. That is when she told me honey cakes were her son's most favorite treat and that I had made them exactly as she had those many years ago.

'When we left she gave each a mighty hug, many teary thank-yous, and a promise that some day she would do us a kindness in return. I believe that is why she was so caring of Father after his accident and so compassionate of us.'

Santa sat in silent fascination. He nodded here and there during the long discourse.

'I should never have doubted that it was a special gift when you gave it last Christmas,' Bretta finished, eyes downturned.

Santa chuckled and winked, making her smile. He then turned to Jonathan. Santa's gaze was kindly, but Jonathan twisted uncomfortably nonetheless.

'I-I-I… you…,' Jonathan stammered and looked down at his feet. Still looking down, he said, 'You have been here long and you have so many houses to visit. Hadn't you better be about it?'

Santa smiled. When Jonathan looked up, his eyes met that smile. It was a shining smile, brimming with magnificence. 'Have no fear, young man,' Santa said. 'I shall visit every household this night and have time to spare. But have you nothing to say to me? How have you enjoyed the toys I left under your tree last year?'

'Toys?…' Jonathan groped through his memory trying to remember which of his toys were gifts from Grammy, which were from his mother, and which were Santa's gifts. 'I… I liked them all… I think.'

Santa drew his lips into a wizened smile. He raised one eyebrow and nodded. Turning abruptly to the others he said, 'Enough of Christmases past! Let us celebrate Christmas present!'

He hopped up, still clenching his pipe in his teeth. He produced a pair of spectacles and perched them on his nose.

'Now, let me see what I have in my bag for this fine family, this wonderful family.' He reached into the red sack at his foot and drew out a four-foot Christmas tree rooted in a bucket.

Jonathan's eyes nearly popped out of their sockets. 'How did you… the bag is so short… and not a branch is bent or broken!'

Jonathan started walking forward but I grabbed his hand. 'Don't go gaping in his sack, Jonathan. Besides being rude, you will discover nothing from it. Anyway, it is time to dress the tree.'

The ornaments we made were retrieved from their shelf and laid out on the table. As we assembled the ornaments, Santa leaned into the hearth, looking up the chimney.

'It is time, my helpers! I hope you are ready,' he shouted and hopped pack quickly. An elf came tumbling out of the fireplace followed by six more in quick succession. Their entrance brought a cloud of black soot into the room. Santa faced away, took a huge breath, and blew the cloud and remnants of ash on the elves clothing back up the chimney. The fire flared causing the elves to rush behind Mister Claus.

Santa turned and signaled for them to make final preparations. The elves produced musical instruments from bags and leather cases about them and began to tune. A harp, two shawms, a raquet, a sacbut, and a portative organ were carefully adjusted and tested with a scale or two. The elf at the portative organ cleared his throat causing the others to finish their riffs. He bobbed his head four times and then did the music begin!

The first tune was 'Past Three O'Clock', and such a lively rendition I have never heard before or since. We had no choice but to dance and sing as we decorated the tree. We reached the last line in the chorus, '…past three o'clock on a cold and frosty morning, past three o'clock, good morrow masters all', and Father put the last ornament on the tree.

'It must truly be past three o'clock by this time,' Jonathan said and all of the elves broke out in jolly, high-pitched laughter.

Then Santa's merry musicians began the introduction of a slower tune. The smooth melody and harmony gave us to know the title without a doubt: 'O Christmas Tree.' As we sang. Santa reached into his bag again and brought out small, lighted candles. Each one was encased in a delicate globe of blown glass. He attached them one by one to the tips of the branches. Before long the tree was fully lit with the fairy lights. Santa stepped back and joined us in singing 'Gather Around the Christmas Tree' accompanied by the elves singing in harmony. As we concluded the carol, Jonathan took my tree-top angel in his hands and Father lifted him so he could place it.

'…Every bough has a burden now
They are gifts of love for us, we trow,
For Christ is born His love to show
And give good gifts to men below.
Hosanna, Hosanna, Hosanna, Hosanna in the highest

Before the last note faded, Santa hopped again to his sack and bent to dig inside. 'Good gifts indeed, my lovely family, my beautiful family. Ho-ho-ho, ha-ha! The gifts this year are a bit different, but special nonetheless!

'Youngest first, I always say,' Santa said carrying an oddly-shaped package decorated in bright reds and greens. 'Elsa, smallest and most dear, how I respect and adore you. You have taken the things you have learned in life and used them to bring joy to others. You are deserving of a most precious gift.'

Elsa tore the paper and brought out six small books. Three were titled 'Little Red

Riding Hood', 'Sleeping Beauty', and 'Puss in Boots', all three written by Charles Perrault. The other three were identical but for the titles: 'Le Petit Chaperon rouge', 'La Belle au bois dormant', and 'Le Maître chat ou le Chat botté'.

Elsa leaned close to Santa's ear and whispered, 'I can't read. And I don't think these three are in English at all.'

Santa laughed his jolly laugh. Several of the elves who were close enough to hear twittered a high-pitched laugh as well. 'The books aren't the present, my dear. They are only the opening. I give to you the gift of friendship,' He winked at Elsa and waived his hand dismissively. 'Bretta will help you learn to read them.'

'But...' Bretta began, however Mister Claus had already turned to his bag again, having directed the elves to accompany the festivities with another jig. He stood with a large, lumpy bundle and fairly danced to me, holding it above his head. He lowered it into my hands. 'To you, Mother, I give more work! HO, HO-HO!'

I curtsied and opened the present without tearing the paper. Within, I found squares of the most beautifully colored fabric. They were tied in bundles of like colors, designs, and prints. There was one square larger than the others printed with the image of a dove in the center. There was also a very large piece folded and tied. 'Oh, what a beautiful quilt this will make!' I exclaimed. I turned to Mister Claus. 'It's a medallion quilt isn't it? Why I can imagine it already! Oh, I would wish for a layer of wadding to give it bulk, though. And perhaps a quilting frame...'

I was suddenly horrified that I may have sounded ungrateful by having asked for more than was given. Santa, however, only laughed.

'Missus McCullough has a quilting frame that is, at present, unoccupied,' he said with a comical twitch of his eyebrows. 'She also has a large stock of wadding she may never use herself! I talked with her this very night at midnight and she said she would be happy to work with you on the quilting.'

'Wait!' Jonathan interrupted. 'You came to *us* at midnight!'

'GLORY, Jonathan,' said Santa in an exasperated tone. 'You are so intent on keeping track of time for me. Satisfy yourself in the thought that time waits for *me* this night!'

Santa turned and looked at Bretta. 'However did I get out of order? Bretta must be next, of course!' He turned to his bag and found that the eldest elf had already gotten Bretta's gift and was holding it up. 'Why thank you Master Harles.'

Santa turned to the family and said in a stage whisper, 'He's a clever one, is Master

Harles. Couldn't do this without him.' In a louder voice he said, 'Bretta, if you please.' He bowed, handing the present to her. 'This one will last a lifetime. Use it well.'

Bretta opened the gift as I did, saving the paper. Her eyes flew wide. She lifted out two cloth-bound books, a slate, and two pieces of chalk. 'I going to school! I'M GOING TO SCHOOL!' she shouted and danced around the room, hugging the books and slate to her.

'You *want* to go to school?' Jonathan asked in an incredulous tone. Bretta didn't hear.

She rushed to Santa and embraced him with all her strength. I went to Father and leaned to his side. He put his arm around my shoulders. Neither of us could bring ourselves to smile, however. We knew the expense of attending school did not end with books and slate.

Bretta noticed our worried looks. The joy in her eyes softened. 'Santa, I'm afraid I cannot accept this gift. It would bring a hardship.'

'Bretta, dear Bretta,' Santa said with a chuckle, 'you didn't think Father Christmas would bring woe wrapped up in paper and a bow did you? Keep those books and slate safe and by the time the new semester starts, we will see what is possible.'

Master Harles tapped him on the shoulder with a rather large package. 'Why yes, good sir, it is time for Father's present.'

Father had seated himself at the table out of weariness from standing. Mister Claus set the present on the table in front of him. Father tore the paper, revealing a wooden box constructed of spaced slats and netting. Father turned it about, looking at every side.

'It's a trap of some sort, isn't it?' he asked, not taking his eyes from the box.

'Yes. Study it well, for you will be making quite a few as your business grows.' Santa's eyes twinkled. 'It is a lobster trap.'

'Oh, no. What should I do with lobster? No one has cared to dine on them for years,' Father said in a disappointed tone. I tried to signal to him to accept the gift gracefully. He apparently didn't see. 'Lobster is the poor man's chicken. They used to pile up on the shores many years ago and were eaten in quantity by the destitute until they got sick of them!'

Santa smiled and winked to his elves. Turning to Father, he said, 'That merchantman in town who gave you Jonathan's slicker... he would like to move his family here from Canada. Ask him if he would attempt to sell lobster as a delicacy to the rich.'

Father sputtered, 'B-but…'

'Ask him,' Santa said, 'and tell him this: ten cents a lobster and not a penny less!'

Father finally laughed, throwing up his hands. 'I yield! As preposterous as it seems, I will follow your instructions!'

Santa turned to Jonathan. He addressed the youngest of the six elves without taking his gaze from the child, 'Master Bartholomew, would you please bring Jonathan his present?'

The smallest elf set down his shawm, hopped over to the hearth, popped up the chimney, and returned with a present in short order. The present was wrapped in deep blue and tied with a white ribbon. Bartholomew handed Jonathan the present.

Santa's eyes never left Jonathan as the boy opened the present.

Inside, Jonathan found fifty-five toy soldiers and fifty-five pirates; one hundred and ten figures in all. Each one was expertly carved and painted. The guns and swords were adorned with gold and silver leaf. The set reminded Jonathan of the one he had seen in his own village store and had pestered his real mother to buy.

Before Jonathan looked up, Santa turned to Father and me and said, 'Well, my dears, I must gather my merry band and be off. It is still Christmas Eve, you know, and we have much to accomplish.'

Jonathan looked up. 'Wait! … Santa … You have nothing else for me? … Nothing… special?' he ended in a whisper.

'Jonathan, you are in a different world now. A mountain of toys, candies, games and clothes would be out of place here. Indeed, it would be…'

'No, that isn't what I meant,' he interrupted Santa. Jonathan looked down at the beautiful toys in his lap. 'I would gladly give these back in trade for a gift like the others received tonight.'

Santa seemed then to be pleased. He said in a slow, quiet voice, 'Jonathan, to you I give a most precious gift. One not possessed by all, but cherished by those who are blessed with it. To you I give the gift of a mother who will love you till the end of eternity.'

He glanced at me and then back at Jonathan.

'But, Mister Claus,' said Jonathan, 'I… I already have this gift.'

Santa was standing with his elves in front of the sparkling Christmas tree. He smiled his broadest smile. 'You see? You had nothing to fear. I am truly quick in my work, for I have given you a gift before you knew you wanted it!'

With that, he and his elves began to sparkle in reflection of the lights on the tree. The lights grew in intensity and then Santa was gone, taking his company and their trappings with them

⤳

The next morning when we awoke, Jonathan was gone.

His magnificent array of sailors and pirates were left in the crumpled paper they were presented in and were stuffed under the girls' sleeping palate. Under the tree we found his present to us. It was wrapped in woven grasses that he had dyed red and green.

He had taken everything else that was his, leaving nothing but his memory.

CHAPTER 8
Black Peter's Assault

Christmas morning.

I opened my eyes already knowing Jonathan was gone. The glow of the morning sun revealed details of our one-room cabin in etchings of deep purple and black. I saw the children's sleeping palate with two mounds instead of three, confirming what I already knew.

A dream had come to me last night. A most vivid dream. So strong was its impact on my mind that I have no doubt it was the true account of what became of Jonathan.

I remember feeling excited and pleased with the wonders of Santa Claus' visit as I lay down to sleep Christmas night. However, as soon as my head touched the pillow, I fell into a deep slumber.

The dream came to me almost immediately. I floated out of my body and drifted through the solid beams of our roof, through the layer of earth and sod above. As a leaf caught in a wild tempest, I was blown high into the sky. I traveled west, away from the sea. Beneath me rolled waves of tree-covered hills, dark in the night. I was hurled faster and faster until the earth was but a blur beneath me. After a while, I slowed and descended to the outskirts of a large village. I was approaching a large house painted in stark whites, grays, and black by the waning moon. I slowed even more and passed smoothly through a second storey window. I was in an opulent bedroom dominated by a great four-poster bed, draped with the most delicate lace. My presence drew close to the person in the bed. It was a young lady, face pale and streaked with tears. She tossed restlessly in the bed, never loosening a two-handed grip on a dark stick held fast to her heart.

As I watched, a shadow detached itself from an ingress in the wall and moved toward the bed. The shadow was so inky black, I could not make out the slightest detail within its depths. The shape of a hand and arm emerged from the shadow and plucked the switch from the young woman's grip. Her empty hands convulsed and her features took on such a visage of grief that I would have cried were it possible.

The clock on the mantle began to strike the hour. I could not see the time in the darkness, but found myself counting the chimes: … nine, ten, eleven, twelve!

The black shadow whipped into sudden motion, flying to the ceiling and through it. I was drawn behind, but the chilling apparition moved with frightening speed and I was alone in a matter of moments. My momentum drew me back the way I had come and before long I found myself descending back through the roof of our cabin. Home.

Rather than settling back into my sleeping form, I hovered above the hearth, gazing at the peaceful scene lit by our Christmas tree's fairy lights. Father turned in his sleep and made a barely audible growl. The girls lay motionless, huddled together for warmth on their straw pallet. The third form on that pallet, belonging to Jonathan, stirred. He sat up and looked around in the darkness, listening intently to our breathing.

Jonathan slipped from the tattered cover and crept on silent feet to the table. There he gathered up the toy sailors that were his gift from Santa and quietly slid them under the palate. He reached farther underneath and brought out the present wrapped in died grasses and placed it under the tree.

Jonathan crept from the tree to the palate where Father and I were sleeping. He reached over my form and laid his hand gently on Father's head. Then he bent and kissed me on the cheek. Next he went to the girls. He took Bretta's hand and kissed it and held

Elsa's hand while he kissed her brow. Seeing Elsa's doll, Brunda , in the darkness, he picked it up and tucked it under Elsa's arm.

Turning quickly, he grabbed the pile of clothes that belonged to him, put them all on in layers, and went to the door. Jonathan looked once more around the room before he unlatched the door and slid out into the night.

⌒

I followed his progress north and east as he followed the path that leads to the village. He slowed as he approached the turn to the crossroads. There was a glow coming from around the bend. Moving slowly and cautiously, Jonathan came into view of the crossroads.

There, sitting on the large granite boulder, was Black Peter. His features were illuminated by the light of a burning switch that he held casually in one hand.

'So… 'tis the spoiled child out for a midnight stroll,' he said in his hollow voice. 'Where might your destination be, boy?'

'I need not tell you a thing,' Jonathan said defiantly although his voice shook a little. 'I do not belong to you.'

'Ah, but you could have,' said Black Peter, stepping down from the boulder and waving the burning branch. 'And I would have treated you well. I would have given you back your mother, your toys and clothes, and your splendid home. When you came of age, I would have seen you into an increasingly lucrative profession. You could have had an appallingly successful future.'

Jonathan retreated a step. "It is possible that I will have success without you, you lying murderer.'

Black Peter grimaced with loathing. 'Not a drop of mortal blood has been shed by my hand, even though I have the power to maim and destroy.'

'No! You do NOT,' screamed Jonathan, shaking visibly. He continued in a more controlled voice, 'You don't. You are only able to *cause* misery and murder by the use of others. You whisper in their ears and promise them what they desire most. You convince them that yours is the only way.

'I know now that I listened to you as a child. You would dangle something pretty in front of my eyes and whisper how much happier I'd be if I had it. You would goad me into demanding that I had it. I would fly into a rage if I didn't get my way. And every time this happened, a little bit of me would become yours.

'If it hadn't been for the poor family, I might never have known.'

'But it was my design that you would follow me more eagerly after having been exposed to destitution and want,' said Black Peter in a puzzled tone.

'Well your design didn't work; and do you know why?' Jonathan took a step towards Black Peter. Black Peter stiffened and held up the burning branch as if to ward him off. 'It is because you think you are in control when in fact you are not,' Jonathan continued. 'Have you forgotten who's bidding you were doing in taking me to the poor family?'

Black Peter's face lost all expression, eyebrows arching slightly. His eyes became half-veiled with heavy lids. Black Peter seemed to glide closer to Jonathan, drawing the shadows of the forest behind him.

Jonathan stood frozen in time.

Black Peter slowly raised the burning stick above Jonathan's head. He let it hover there a moment, the wan light reflecting in his cold eyes. Then those evil eyes flew wide and he snapped the switch down into Jonathan's hair.

Flame descended in a globe, encasing the boy.

CHAPTER 9
The Child's Precious Gift

The clock on my dresser drawers chimed six o'clock. It was Christmas morning. My child had been missing since December 5th. I had had no more visions, or should I say 'nightmares', of his whereabouts since that first night. Even so, I still carried the switch that I found on the night of his abduction. I knew it to be some sort of talisman, some sort of key to the horror I had been subjected to; the horror my child had been subjected to.

My mother, of course, thought I was mad.

At any rate, the switch was rarely out of my sight. ... *The switch!* ... I suddenly realized it was not in my hand as it had been every morning since St. Nicholas Day! I searched frantically through the bed covers and looked under and around the bed. It can't have just disappeared! I began to pull the bedclothes from the mattress, throwing them on the floor.

I stopped suddenly. There was a shuffling noise outside my bedroom door. Who could be inside my house this time in the morning on Christmas Day?

My door opened in very slowly. Black fingers leaving a smudge on the white paint. JONATHAN!

He stood there covered from head to bare feet in soot flecked with ashes. He smelled of burnt hair and cloth. I ran to him and knelt to hug him for all I was worth.

Jonathan had come back to me.

Earlier in the season, I had bought a few toys, halfheartedly wrapped them and placed them under the tree. My mother had also brought over a few gaily wrapped boxes in the afternoon of Christmas Eve and sat with me through the long lonely evening.

Lonely no longer! My child had come home!

Jonathan ignored the small pile of presents until evening. The day was spent bathing, choosing clothing to wear, resting, and telling all that had happened since that horrid night he was taken.

I didn't trouble my mind to ponder the truthfulness of the story, although it was curious the parts that matched my dreams. I only cared that my child was home safe. His voice was music in my ears. I had to rest my hands on him constantly, to hold his hands, to brush the hair from his forehead.

We dined on cold roast, corn, turnips and honey cakes and then retired to the parlor where sat the splendid Christmas tree. The small scattering of presents below the lowest boughs danced in the warm light of the fire in the great hearth. Jonathan sat in my lap glancing from me to the presents.

'Don't you want to open them, Jonathan?' I asked.

Jonathan nodded, but didn't get down from my lap. 'Mother, did you tell me that your friend, Missus Flemming, has two daughters?'

'The widow Flemming, poor thing? Why yes. How did you remember this?'

'You were gone for a whole day helping her settle in her house. She was just returned from Iowa.'

'Yes,' I said, 'the family lost everything in their venture. Her mister died in a mishap on the farm leaving her with barely enough to return. My heart goes out to her daughters.'

Jonathan was staring intently at the presents under the tree. He smiled. 'I know who would love to open these much more than me.'

I looked down at him. He continued to stare at the presents as if he could see the Flemming girls opening them right then. Suddenly his eyes focused and his eyebrows rose. 'What is that?'

He hopped down from my lap and ran behind the tree. Propped against the wall was a present wrapped in blue and yellow. I dipped my head in surprise. My presents were wrapped in red and green plaid and Grammy's were white with red ribbons. Where did this one come from?

Jonathan was on his knees opening the present without tearing the paper. He began lifting out the most beautiful figurines, one by one. They were sailors and pirates; one hundred and ten in all. Jonathan lined them up facing one another, laughing heartily as he did.

He leaned slightly toward the hearth. 'Oh, all right. I'll keep them seeing as how you insist! Girls have little interest in sailors at any rate.'

Jonathan saw my quizzical look and laughed again. Quieting to a broad smile, he looked at me with shining eyes.

'Santa gives the most special gifts.'

Epilogue

There is a family living in a fishing village on a rocky northern coast. The family consists of a father, mother, two daughters, and a newborn son.

The father is a fisherman. He is well known for his net designs and is generally acknowledged as the man who began the lobster trade in that area. He works with a Canadian merchant who was at first reluctant to venture into a business exporting such a commodity. Little did either of them know the demand that would be created by their efforts.

The mother keeps their new house in the village, educates her children in the arts of homemaking, and sews. Her quilts in particular are of exquisite design and show a considerate amount of craft. Women from as far away as Rockland come to ask her advice and work in her quilting circles.

The elder daughter is in her second year of primary school. Although she is not the most gifted student in the village school, she does work harder than most and cherishes the education that is her life-long gift.

The younger daughter will attend school when the new semester begins this year. Presently, she is a great help to her mother and to her best friend, Claire. Claire is the daughter of the Canadian merchant who is the business partner of the fisherman father. The girls met on the first day the merchant's family spent in the fishing village. Claire was at first withdrawn and sad because she spoke only French and was afraid she would have no friends in her new home. The fisherman's daughter spoke only English, but had a set of books in both languages giving them common ground. They became fast friends, sitting for hours trading phrases.

The youngest member of the family is the infant, Johnny. He was born several months after the fisherman moved his family into a large, comfortable house in the village. The daughters were delighted and insisted on the name 'John.'

The family owns few possessions they consider dear. Among them is a small, somewhat crude carving of a mother and child. Although the members of the family are unsure whether it is the Madonna and Child that is depicted or a universal representation of mother and child, they consider the work priceless. The eldest daughter says it keeps all other possessions in perspective.

The carving is made of a simple bar of soap.

LaVergne, TN USA
13 October 2009
160649LV00003B/2/P

9 781440 176357